I0453869

NUMBER NINE

THE ADVENTURES OF

JAKE JONES AND RUBY DAULTON

A NOVEL BY JACK RANDOM

CROW DOG PRESS
TURLOCK CA USA

Number Nine:

The Adventures of
Jake Jones and Ruby Daulton

A Novel by Jack Random

Published by
Crow Dog Press
1241 Windsor Court
Turlock CA 95380

ISBN 978-0692471869

NUMBER NINE

THE ADVENTURES OF

JAKE JONES AND RUBY DAULTON

To my wife and love of my life
Julie Marie Bradford
Who has remained by my side these many years
Despite my numerous eccentricities

SCENE 1: HELTER SKELTER

FADE IN:

EXTERIOR SAN FERNANDO VALLEY – ARIEL VIEW
– DAY

Smog and traffic patterns.

The Beatles' REVOLUTION 9 (White Album) begins softly and grows.

INSERT MONTAGE – SOCIAL INSANITY

Charles Manson, Rwanda, OJ Simpson, CNN war footage, demonstrations, traffic jams, crime scenes, sporting events, politicians, scandals, smog, poisoned water, drought, animal cruelty, disease, southern California fires, on and on.

BACK TO SCENE

ZOOM to a woman in a 1967 baby blue Dodge Coronet convertible speeding down a suburban street. This is RUBY DAULTON, 36, a wild woman, exotic dancer, edgy and sexy.

Fade REVOLUTION 9 to HELTER SKELTER (White Album).

When I get to the bottom I go back to the top of the slide
Where I stop and I turn and I go for a ride...

Ruby is intense, worried, with one eye on the rearview mirror. She turns suddenly as she glimpses a blue BMW rounding a corner in the mirror.

....

Ruby kept busy – picking up, wiping down, stacking dishes, emptying ashtrays, rearranging books, anything – to keep from sitting with the men in her living room. They were uninvited guests, a couple of boys from the office. The office was what they called Ruby's place of employment. Customers called it Shotgun Slim's – a stripper bar in the great San Fernando Valley, where the sun always shines, majestic palms sway in the wind and the air is a toxic mix of internal combustion soup.

It was Ruby's birthday but the boys brought nothing but trouble. They sat side by side on the sofa in the living room of her small bungalow, laughing, ball adjusting and back slapping over a televised boxing match between an Italian and a black man. She was reminded of the one question that settled in her mind years ago and, like an unwanted relative, never left: What the fuck am I doing here?

It was a long way from the Land of Oz where Ruby first learned to dream. She knew how she had gotten here. What she did not know and could not have understood if she did was why she had chosen to stay. That old saying: Aint it hard to break those habits set in flesh and blood? She couldn't do it. One day led to the next and she couldn't break the pattern.

The boys were getting too high, too coked up, and too ass kicking buzzed on the combination of televised violence with gin and tonic. A fourth round technical knockout brought them to frenzy and let them down hard. They had little else to do but turn their rabid attentions to the birthday gal. They won their boxing bets but Ruby was the real loser. It gave them a sense of invincibility they had not earned and did not deserve.

As it happened, Ruby had a man. He was the owner of Shotgun Slim's and these boys were supposed to be his friends and partners – brothers in the vocabulary of their sordid business. She knew what they were about. They would use their highs as an excuse for what they fully intended to do. No excuse would be good enough for Ruby: That she was a woman? That she was not physically strong enough to hold them off? Should she take a beating only to suffer the same consequences – only worse?

The truth is she did not like her boyfriend any more than she liked his friends. They were all scumbags – little piggy punks with drugs, money and guns. Unfortunately, Ruby had a need for what they offered and until now a high tolerance for bullshit.

"What the fuck am I doing here?" she asked aloud as they implored her with outstretched paws and sad sack grins to come to them.

"Get your ass in here, you sexy fucking bitch!"

They were pawing their dicks, squeezing their balls, laughing and clapping like wild boars circling a wounded ground hog.

Ruby took account and decided to stay cool. She left herself behind in the kitchen, along with the memories of who she once was: a dumb kid from Kansas, pretty and popular enough to finish third in the race for Homecoming Queen. Sexy Sadie. Protected from all harm, she hid herself in the closet of her mind, safe behind walls of mental concrete and layers of darkness. She walked out of herself and, like Norma Jean becoming Marilyn, she became Ruby Daulton, queen of the dance floor, star of the stage where the silver phallus is always front and center. She struck a pose that never failed to pique a man's interest.

"Tony wouldn't like this," she purred.

Tony was Antonio Menendez, her sometime man and their sometime boss.

"Tony aint gonna hear about it," replied Little Billy. He was a large man with short hair, ruddy complexion, and bulging biceps. He was known at the office as "the muscle." Ruby sensed that he hated the boss as much as she did but Tony was as clueless as a turkey in November.

"Alright then," she said, sliding her hips from side to side like a panther stalking her prey.

"What do you boys want?"

Little Billy grabbed his balls. "Hey, babe, you know what I want!"

He used a remote to pick up some music on the television. They had prepared something special: a mix from The Beatles' White Album, beginning with Birthday.

They say it's your birthday
Happy birthday to you!

Ruby waited as long as she could before beginning the slow, lingering movements known as the tease. She had decided to play along and as long as she played the boys would be content. They liked to watch. They liked the anticipation almost as much as what followed. Maybe more.

Yes we're going to a party party

She removed her shoes and was beginning to remove her shirt when the music shifted to Sexy Sadie. Ruby loved Sexy Sadie. It meant more to her than they could ever imagine. She began to move to the rhythm inside. She closed her eyes and began to dance – not the cheap, over-rehearsed dance of the stripper but the dance of the muses in ancient mythology. She danced and the muses wept. She closed her eyes and thought of Dorothy and Kansas and the wizard who was not a wizard and ruby-red shoes on a yellow brick road. She spun and danced and she imagined fields of golden grass, waves of amber grace, green hills covered with wild flowers and poppies – glistening white poppies from here to the end of time. She closed her eyes, tapped her heels, and flew away on the wings of angelic beings.

Sexy Sadie, how did you know?
The world was waiting just for you

When she awakened with a jolt, everything had changed. Sexy Sadie had given way to a blaring *Happiness is A Warm Gun*. The transition was sudden and disturbing. It was an omen as surely as a crow in the morning or crossing the path of a black cat under a full moon. It was snake eyes and a dead man's hand. It was a dead skunk in the middle of the road.

"This is wrong," she said.

The boys were not persuaded. To them it was written in the stars. It was manifest. It was destiny. As far as they were concerned, happiness *was* a warm gun and a sexy woman to help it along.

"Dance, baby! Take it off!"

Ruby turned to the windows at the front of her little bungalow and thought she saw the momentary glimpse of a moving shadow.

"Antonio's here," she said.

"Bullshit, baby, he's tied up."

I need a fix 'cause I'm going down

Ruby danced but it was no longer the dance of the swans. It was back to the old routine. It was the familiar dance of a stripper on a long and lonely night when men too tired, too drunk, too high and too excited to think pawed the stage and clamored for more. The smell of sweat and spent ejaculations stifled the air and choked away any beauty and grace in the dancer's performance. It was nasty and dirty and as phony as the smile on a real estate broker's face.

The boys were not content with the pace of Ruby's tease. They rushed the improvised stage of her living room, ripped the clothes from her body, and forced her to her knees as Ruby kicked, scratched and fought but refused to scream. She would not give them that satisfaction. She would face the demons as she always had. She would be strong – quietly defiant.

A crash at the door, felt more than heard, interrupted them at the height of their excitement. It was Antonio. He was the picture of a jealous man who was tipped off by someone with a personal interest.

Happiness is a warm gun
Bang-bang, shoot-shoot!

Ruby somehow managed to grab her clothes and move to the back of the room. The boys, holding their pants, were trying to explain how it was all Ruby's fault. She was a tease. He knew that. She had the power and she used it. She seduced them. They were men like any other men. What could they do?

Little Billy saw the rage in Tony's eyes and knew their words were a waste. It was the rage of a man betrayed by those he had considered his friends, his partners and his brothers. They rambled on if only to buy time and to let the rage gradually disperse. Maybe they could get out with their lives.

"She'll get hers," mumbled Antonio. It was all Ruby needed to hear.

Little Billy went for his gun first. It was a futile gesture and he knew it, the desperate last act of a dead man. Antonio brought the wrath of jealousy and betrayal, the hammer of vengeance down upon their heads. He emptied two handguns, reloaded, and made a point of blowing their faces off.

Ruby escaped. She dashed out the back, ran around

the corner, past Antonio's blue BMW, jumped in her convertible and drove away just as Tony emerged, splattered in blood and looking for his ultimate revenge.

The television survived and played on.

Helter skelter helter skelter
Will you won't you want me to make you
I'm coming down fast but don't let me break you

Helter skelter helter skelter
Tell me tell me tell me the answer
You may be a lover but you aint no dancer

Look out, helter skelter helter skelter
Look out!

SCENE 2: JAKE JONES

FADE IN:

EXTERIOR AGRONOMICAL NOWHERE – ARIEL
VIEW – NEARING SUNSET

ZOOM to Ruby in a baby blue convertible, hair died
seven shades of green, flying in the wind.

The Beatles' REVOLUTION 9 fades to WHY DON'T
WE DO IT IN THE ROAD? (White Album)

ZOOM out to ARIEL VIEW and back in to a man in
khakis and plaid work shirt, reclining on a log under a
lonely oak alongside the road, face covered by a straw
hat and an open book on his chest.

This is JAKE JONES, 36, a mixed breed (Navaho-Irish)
with distinctive native features, long hair tied in a
single braid. He is reading Leonard Peltier's *Prison
Writings*.

The Beatles' YER BLUES (White Album) is heard ("Yes,
I'm lonely...") as flies and gnats buzz around his head.

Yes I'm lonely wanna die
Yes I'm lonely wanna die
If I aint dead already
Girl you know the reason why

Jake stirs, swiping the bugs away with his book, stands, stretches and strikes the hitchhikers pose.

YER BLUES fades out as DON'T PASS ME BY (White Album) comes to the fore.

Don't pass me by don't make me cry don't make me blue
'Cause you know darling I love only you

In the distance, a baby blue convertible kicks up dust, speeding toward Jake's hitching post. Ruby waves as she passes him by but fishtails to a stop half a mile down the road. Jake remains where he is as Ruby slowly backs up to meet him.

. . . .

Back on the Rez he was known as Grey Hawk but the rest of the world knew him as Jake Jones. Like many Indians, he had two names: one for the native community and another for the world at large. He considered Grey Hawk his true name, the name that would welcome him to the Overworld, while Jake Jones was a concession to the white European society that killed, tortured and enslaved his people in the name of manifest destiny. It made it easier to walk among them. Not that he held a grudge but he never for a moment forgot who he was and the world was teeming with reminders.

The world was changing. As he traveled he met more and more white people who claimed Indian bloodlines – mostly Cherokee. He would endeavor gently to remind these people that if you had not walked the red road you could not claim its heritage.

He left Third Mesa, where he had studied the ways of the ancestors with a gifted medicine man, nine months prior. He was a pilgrim, a seeker in search of destiny and adventure. Like so many of his people – and, as he would learn, so many of all Americans – he was lost in a world dominated by mass media imagery and technology. He felt isolated and disillusioned in the modern world but he was determined not to return to the safe refuge of the Rez, the relative comfort of the ancient rituals, until he had discovered some secret knowledge or wisdom that would illuminate a new path for him if not for his people.

His journey had taken him on a circular route, beginning at the site of the Sand Creek Massacre in southeastern Colorado, where the spirits of the dead still cried out for justice. He moved on to the sacred Chiricahua Mountains of the Apache, where the face of Cochise, gazing at the heavens, marks his unknown grave. He traveled on to Indian Territory, where he paid tribute at the grave of the Apache spirit guide, warrior and healer, Geronimo. He visited the National Indian Museum in Anadarko and witnessed the success of the modern Cherokee Nation. From Oklahoma, he had gone north to smoke and sweat with the political prisoner of the modern day siege at Wounded Knee, Leonard Peltier.

Peltier was strong, steady and hopeful but Jake sensed that he understood: He would remain in prison as a testament to the white man's unending spirit of revenge even against those he victimized.

He laid eyes on the White Buffalo in northern Minnesota, original land of the Lakota nation, and felt the closeness of the spirit world. From Minnesota, he went west to the Little Big Horn, where he felt the spirits of Sitting Bull and Crazy Horse, as well as the glorified butcher of the Indian peoples: Colonel George Armstrong Custer.

The final destination of his pilgrimage, completing a great circle on the North American continent, was the Wounded Knee Memorial. Against a backdrop of corruption, infighting and extreme poverty at Pine Ridge and Rosebud, the memorial itself all but broke his spirit. Only fifty paces from Wounded Knee Hill, where the remains of Big Foot and the Ghost Dancers lay, stood the eternal symbol of the white man's conquest of native lands: The Sacred Heart Church. He learned that the Holy Rosary Catholic Church was the owner of the most sacred land in Native American history. It stirred a rage in him that was not easily conquered or forgotten but it eventually gave way to a profound sorrow.

He went into the Black Hills as Crazy Horse had to cry for a vision in the Lakota way. He fasted seven days for an understanding of how it had come to be and what could be done to restore the balance of forces. Amidst visions of darkness, massacre and betrayal, the answer came to him in the form of the crow and the coyote, who would become his spirit animals: They told him nothing could be done to correct the great wrongs of the past. It fell to him to seek his own path, to find peace with the many as well as the one that dwelled within his self. He understood their message but it brought him no solace. It rather fed his restless spirit, his sense of homelessness and alienation.

Since then, he had wandered through the land as a beggar would with no greater needs or thoughts than his hunger and thirst, his need to survive in a land that was neither caring nor indifferent. He took odd jobs – fixing cars, washing dishes, menial labor – while working his way from town to town, down the coast from the Great Northwest to Southern California, where now he sat by the side of the road, waiting for destiny to play its hand.

He was somewhere near Weed Patch outside of Bakersfield, where he had finished his day's labor gathering grapes from a corporate vineyard. Having already sold his car for traveling money (a good deal at $250), he was down to his last fifty bucks, hot, tired and hungry. He passed on a ride to town. It somehow felt better being out in the middle of agronomical nowhere where he could breathe. At least, he could eat some grapes and bathe in a nearby irrigation canal. If he had to sleep outdoors, he preferred the open skies to the concrete wasteland of Bakersfield. If ever there was a land the gods forgot the city of Bakersfield was at its center.

Jake looked around and laughed. Was this what the Great Spirit had in mind for Grey Hawk? Was this where he needed to be in order to find the answers he sought? He glared into a bright unforgiving sky and felt his stomach churn. Grapes as a source of sustenance were getting old and his bowels were experiencing an uprising. He needed a cheeseburger so bad he was daydreaming of Dairy Queens with waitresses on roller skates, serving imitation ice cream, root beer floats, banana splits and sundaes thick with fudge, nuts and sprinkles, with a ruby red cherry on top.

He lifted his nose to the air and breathed deeply, sifting through dust and dry heat for a taste of fresh air beyond the sweat that clung to his skin like a coat of dry wax. He had no idea where he was going. All roads seemed to run in the wrong directions. He sat on a log, opened his book and waited, waited, waited.

"It's time," he said aloud to no one but the wisp of white clouds drifting high above, "for the world to take a turn."

A crow cawed in the blue highways of his mind. A dog with the eyes of a coyote stared at him from the back of a pickup. The microcosmic world of gnats and subatomic creatures began to take on third and fourth dimensions. A face emerged from the oak tree under which he sat. The hot, dry air came to life: Patterns and fields of energy and particles of light leaving visible traces in the palpable ectoplasm.

Suddenly, he sensed what Einstein must have seen. Suddenly, he saw what Crazy Horse called the real life beyond this life. Drifting in and out of conscious mind, stealing glimpses of a gods' eye view, he saw the possibility of a modern day Prometheus bringing fire to the land of darkness.

When he came out of it, it was approaching sunset. He scanned the horizon, ate some grapes and laid back down for a nap. Brushing away some gnats and wiping the layers of greasy sweat from his eyes, a car suddenly appeared in the distance, kicking up dust, blaring music and traveling twice the speed of sound.

He stood to assume the hitchhiker's pose. It was a classic light blue convertible driven by a mad woman with wild green hair flowing in the wind. She smiled and waved as she blew past him like a shooting star or a desert mirage.

Jake took it well, shaking his head and sitting back down to his book, as the car abruptly skidded and grinded to a halt well down the road. He watched it edge backward to where he sat, half expecting her to dust him again.

"How long have you been here?" she asked.

He pulled out a pocket watch.

"Nine hours," he answered.

"What are you reading?" she asked.

"Leonard Peltier's *Prison Writings*," he replied.

"What page?"

He glanced down at the book, open in his hand. "Page 27."

"Damn," she replied with an expression between a smile and resignation.

"Get the fuck in, pilgrim."

He did not have to be asked twice.

Number nine, number nine, number nine...

SCENE 3: DESTINY

FADE IN:

EXTERIOR SLEEPY TIME MOTEL – NIGHT

The Beatles' I'M SO TIRED (White Album) plays as a neon sign, featuring a blinking bear with a silly nightcap, flashes on and off.

> *I'm so tired*
> *I haven't slept a wink*
> *I'm so tired*
> *My mind is on the blink*
> *I wonder should I get up and fix myself a drink?*
> *No, no, no…*

REVOLUTION 9 (White Album) plays briefly.

The door of a motel room: number nine.

INTERIOR SMALL MOTEL ROOM – NIGHT

I'M SO TIRED resumes as Jake sleeps in boxer shorts atop the single queen size bed. A bag with a Dairy Queen logo and a soda are on a side table. Candles are lit and light seeps in from the adjoining bathroom along with the sound of a SHOWER.

The shower stops and Jake struggles to awaken from deep sleep. Ruby emerges wrapped in a towel. Her hair is black. I'M SO TIRED fades into I WILL (White Album).

> *Who knows how long I've loved you?*
> *You know I love you still*
> *Will I wait a lonely lifetime?*

Seen through Jake's eyes, slowly coming into focus, Ruby speaks as if from a distance.

                    RUBY
          Do you believe in destiny?

Jake nods and the song answers for him.

> *If you want me to, I will*

Ruby lets the towel drop to the floor, revealing her exquisite form.

....

Somewhere around these parts (maybe on this same desolate road), James Dean took his final drive, sacrificing what remained of a promising career for a place amongst the legends of Hollywood lore. Ruby felt his anguish, his hunger for raw experience, his eagerness to take it to the edge (even if it meant diving into the abyss) and she pressed the pedal to the floor.

It felt good to get out of the city. It felt good to be going nowhere and getting there fast. For the moment, she had no worries except rounding the next corner and negotiating the next curve. She wanted to test the fates. She wanted to walk on the edge and not look back, like James Dean and Marilyn Monroe, like Jim Morrison and Janis Joplin, like Jimi Hendrix and Tupac Shakur, like River Phoenix and Kurt Kobain. After everything that had happened, after the sum total of her miserable life ended up on a lonely road to nowhere, she wanted to fly. She wanted to take the final step off the ledge of Grand Canyon. She wanted to test the fates.

Ruby believed in destiny as an anarchist believes in freedom, as a preacher believes in prayer or as a writer believes in words. She believed that James Dean was meant to die young and free on some desolate road, that a man was meant to set foot on the moon on July 20, 1969, that the Japanese were preordained to attack Pearl Harbor on December 7, 1941, and that two planes were destined to crash into the twin towers on September 11, 2001.

Ruby believed that it was possible to tap the source of future events. She believed that it was possible to prevent tragedies or to secure greatness by attending to signs and omens. She believed the gods were not unkind; that they provided signs and omens to those who paid attention. She was a student of the oracles: tarot, astrology, tealeaves and the I Ching. Her latest fixation was the study of numbers and to that end she carried the book *Numerology for Idiots* everywhere. Her working theory was that everything of importance – historically or personally, for good or for evil – was somehow connected to the number nine.

Ruby also believed in free will and found it no philosophical dilemma. What was the purpose of divining the future if you were powerless to alter it? She believed that those who possessed the knowledge and talent to foresee future events had the power to alter those events.

Rounding a curve, she skidded off the side of the road, kicking up dust, reminding herself of her own mortality. She lightened her foot on the pedal and smiled at the sight of a lone hitchhiker alongside the road. It was an enigmatic picture, like a desert coyote in midtown Manhattan. Was it a sign or an omen? She waved as she swept by but continued to watch him in the rearview mirror. When he did not look after her, she slammed on the brakes and skidded to a stop. Throwing her into reverse, she eased back for a closer look, careful to maintain enough distance that she could dust him if she decided he was not worth the risk.

The universe had changed in the world of the hitchhiker. They once represented the spirit of freedom and adventure. Now they were mostly outlaws and desperados. Ruby was sympathetic but she was also mindful of the risk. The modern world gave birth to too many deranged individuals bent on sharing their pain. This was a different sort of hitchhiker. His features were distinctly Native American and he looked like the hull of a fishing trawler, coated with dirt and layers of sweat. She noticed that he was holding a book in his left hand and she took it as a positive sign.

"What are you reading?" she asked in a high

pitched voice that was considered by some as sweet as cotton candy, by others as charming as a squeaky hinge.

"Peltier's *Prison Writings*," he replied.

She mulled it over. A reference to prison gave her pause but she had heard of Peltier, a Lakota Indian wrongly imprisoned – or so they said.

"What page?"

He glanced down at the book, still open in his hand. "Page 27."

Ruby smiled. She glanced at the dashboard clock. It read 8:01.

"Get in."

In the world of numerology, the numbers 801 and twenty-seven convert to the number nine. In Ruby's newfound creed, it was an undeniable sign of destiny. She was meant to be on this road at this particular moment in time and so was he. They were destined to come together in the mystical hour of twilight, at a pivotal time in each of their lives, to share the road ahead – for better or for worse.

"What's your name, stranger?"

"Jake," he replied.

"Just get out of prison?"

He laughed. "Sort of."

Jake was suddenly aware of his appearance. He was dead tired, hungry, and his skin was crawling with microscopic multitudes of unknown origin. He was in no mood for idle conversation yet he recognized the obligation of his good fortune. Here was a strikingly attractive woman – even if she did have green hair – and he for all appearances was a bum.

"Got a last name, pilgrim?"

"Jones."

Ruby was working the numbers in her mind. In numerology, each letter has an assigned number:

1	2	3	4	5	6	7	8	9
A	B	C	D	E	F	G	H	I
J	K	L	M	N	O	P	Q	R
S	T	U	V	W	X	Y	Z	

"Jake is nine," she said. "Oh my God, Jones is nine! Jesus," she said, staring into Jake's tired eyes, "you're a triple nine!" She checked the math, scribbling in her book to confirm what she already knew. His first name totaled nine, his last name nine, and all multiples of nine break down to nine. It is one of great mysteries of theoretical and phenomenological mathematics. In numerology, of course, while multiples of eleven are power numbers, multiples of nine are destiny: completion, climax, culmination, epiphany, and rebirth.

Ruby Daulton was also nine and, since all multiples of nine are nine, Jake Jones and Ruby Daulton combined were nine. Nines were everywhere! Nines were wild!

Jake had encountered numerology before but not so much as a religion as a curiosity. There were many ways to see the future and he had had a hand at many of them: crying for a vision, sun dance, sweat lodge, tossing stones, and gazing into the eyes of a crow. He had the gift of prophetic dreams. He had seen much of the future and much of the past but he had never seen what he wanted to see. He had not found the answer to the proverbial question: How do I get back home?

Ruby examined him with new eyes, seeing beyond

the filth and grime that disguised his true being. She liked what she saw. Everything was good. Everything was right. Here in the middle of absolute nowhere, the sun setting in a western sky, she may have finally found the first genuinely good man in her life. In the oracle of Ruby's creed, destiny had cast its stone, the fates had planted their magic seeds, all was right on heaven and earth, and theirs was a meeting of celestial divination.

"Let's get you a shower," she said, throwing her in gear and burning down the highway, headed for the next town and the first motel they came across. Her car's name was Sadie Mae: Sadie = eleven, Mae = eleven, Sadie Mae = 22: pure power.

Jake was speechless. Never had he made such an impression on a woman and never had a woman made such an impression on him. He had an acute need for solid food, sleep and cleansing but, for a while, she was all that occupied his mind. Even at the speed of sound, Ruby was all he could see. All he could hear was: Number nine, number nine, number nine... She went on and on about probability, random chance and the oracles of divination, but all he could hear was: Number nine, number nine, number nine...

"It doesn't matter what you believe," she said. "You could chart the stars, have your palms read, consult Tarot, or toss the I Ching sticks, it all leads to the same conclusion: It's destiny."

Jake was suddenly overcome with undeniable fatigue and allowed himself to drift until he arrived in that grey area where dream and reality are one. He thought of something a spirit guide once told him:

"In a world soft as butterflies, as violent as the

raging sea, there's no such thing as random chance."

Sacred spiral, helter-skelter, forces of the ancients, flight through the windows of perception to the world within and beyond, held by slender threads of time and space, at one with the Great Spirit, past and future, all and the void, weightless, senseless and breathless in the infinite chain of matter and mystery. The world was turning at last.

Ruby saw the neon light of a Sleepy Time Motel and knew she had arrived. She checked in under the names Jake and Ruby Jones, insisted on cabin #9 and paid cash. The desk clerk gave her a wink. She shook Jake awake, handed him the key, and explained that she was off to grab some burgers.

"Don't forget to shower," she said over her shoulder.

Jake stared after her until he located his center and remembered where he was and how he came to be there. The key in his hand read: number nine. He became aware of a foul odor and looked around for its source before he realized it was emanating from his own body.

Entering the motel room, he stumbled into the shower and let the cool water cleanse him, washing away seven layers of gritty, sweat-solidified waste. He wondered how a man in his condition could be so fortunate.

Who was this wild woman who spoke of destiny and challenged his imagination? Where was she headed and what was she running from? Was it really destiny or just random chance? In a world as soft as butterflies, as violent as a raging sea, was there really any difference?

He collapsed on the bed and fell through the vortex back into the world of dreams. He saw Ruby in a red dress on a stage of amber light. Men with eyes wide open gaped as she let the dress slip from her shoulders.

Who was she and what was she running from? He heard music and the sound of running water. He saw light from above and struggled to reach it. He saw her face like a diamond in a sea of common stones. He heard music, sweet and soft.

> *For if I ever saw you*
> *I didn't catch your name*
> *But it never really mattered*
> *I will always feel the same*

Ruby emerged from the bathroom wrapped in a towel. Through the haze of his awakening, he could see that she had dyed her hair black. Who was she? What was she running from? It no longer mattered. In a life of hardship, in a universe full of darkness, she was the most beautiful woman he had ever encountered. She was an enchantress and a saint.

"Do you believe in destiny?" she asked.

He nodded and let the music answer.

> *If you want me to, I will*

Ruby let the towel drop to the floor.

> *Love you forever and forever*
> *Love you with all my heart*
> *Love you whenever we're together*
> *Love you when we're apart*

SCENE 4: RANDOM CHANCE

FADE IN:

INTERIOR TELEVISION SCREEN – NIGHT

The Beatles' EVERYBODY'S GOT SOMETHING TO HIDE EXCEPT ME AND MY MONKEY (White Album) plays as we see a boxed photograph of Ruby Daulton displayed alongside a talking head with the CNN logo and scroll bar below. The caption reads: "Person of Interest."

> *The deeper you go the higher you fly*
> *The higher you fly the deeper you go*
> *So come on!*

EXTERIOR DAIRY QUEEN PAY PHONE – NIGHT

Fade MONKEY as Ruby talks on the phone. We hear bits of her conversation.

RUBY
I can't do that … Listen, I need some help …

EXTERIOR MOUNTAIN ROAD, RUBY – NIGHT

Jake in the passenger seat, top down beneath a bright moon, Ruby drives up a winding road as the radio blares WHY DON'T WE DO IT IN THE ROAD? (White Album).

INTERIOR CABIN OF AN 18 WHEELER

A trucker, barreling down the same mountain road, steps on the brakes with no effect. We hear REVOLUTION 9 ("Number 9, number 9, number 9...") as the truck picks up speed and the trucker sounds his HORN.

EXTERIOR MOUNTAIN ROAD, ABOVE

A runaway truck veers into the middle of the road as Ruby's convertible approaches the same curve ahead. They appear destined to meet.

Ruby sees a white post reading: Mile 9. She pulls off the road at a lookout just as the truck barrels by and smashes into a sandy runaway truck ramp down the road.

....

In the microcosmic world, entities swim about in a gelatinous muck, moved by their liquid or gaseous surroundings, guided by unseen electrical impulses and unknown encoded tendencies. The patterns are beyond our earthbound grasp, like the courting dance of jellyfish, seemingly random and without intent, but when an entity nears its perfect mate, the two are drawn together like yin and yang, Orion and Sirius, Anthony and Cleopatra, or Tristan and Isolde. Two become one, forever interwoven, joined at the hip in a perpetual dance of destiny.

If not for the cerebral cortex, as it is in the microcosmic world so would it be for human nature. We would all find our perfect mates, dance in flowing harmony and claim eternal bliss.

So it seemed for Jake Jones and Ruby Daulton: If ever a match in heaven was made, at this moment in the cosmos, they were it. Her perfect breasts, nipples erect from leather thoughts, were soft and white. He caressed them in his mind though his thoughts were pure with wonder. He caressed them in the flesh and his spirit left his body, soaring through the ectoplasm of electromagnetic dreams.

She moved to him until their bodies locked like the socket and the plug, an electromagnetic coupling, matter and antimatter, like a Chopin duet or the final chapter of Joyce's Ulysses.

Jake lived in the moment almost completely. It was not the result of a conscious decision but a birthright and one of many eccentricities that served to accentuate sensual-sexual pleasure. Their bodies tingled with an excitation of a kind Ruby had never before experienced. From the caverns of her mind reemerged the song that spurred the lust of Tony's boys, sealed their gruesome fate, and turned the wheel of destiny.

When I hold you in my arms
And I feel my finger on your trigger
I know no one can do me no harm

Because happiness is a warm gun

"Forever!" she cried out from the summit of delight. They were swimming the seven seas, soaring over Grand Canyon, diving into the infinite abyss.

"You and I will live ... forever!"

Was it true love? It is a question neither Jake nor Ruby could ever answer but it was a moment of pure bliss and it would pass for love as long as they let it be so. For all they knew – for all any of us know – that is what love is: a willingness to suspend logical belief in favor of the eternal heart.

Exhausted, they lay side by side, basking in the scent of their liquid love, when Ruby turned to him and smiled. She had an epiphany.

"Ruby," she said. "Ruby Daulton."

It was only then that Jake realized he did not know her name. He could not recall having heard or seen it written but it was as if he already knew.

"And it's my birthday."

Without a second thought, he pulled a turquoise stone on a leather thong from around his neck and handed it to her. It was a gift from a wise woman in Santa Fe. They had helped each understand and accept the mystery of their separate journeys.

"Happy birthday, Ruby Daulton."

Holding the stone in her hands, it brought tears to her eyes for reasons she could never understand. For the first time since she was a child, she cried without apology or remorse. It was the most precious gift she had ever received.

"Baby," she said finally, "I've got to level with you and after I do, if you want to turn your back and walk away, I swear I won't say a word."

Leaving nothing to the imagination, Ruby explained what had happened and why she was on the run. Her boyfriend was a mafia psychopath and she was a common stripper. The boys were scumbags who decided to take advantage. By the grace of god she was still alive. Raped, bruised and wanted by the law but she was still alive. Jake listened quietly before offering the obvious advice.

"You didn't do anything wrong," he said. "Turn yourself in."

"I've got history, baby. They know me at the LAPD. Tony knows that. He was counting on it. He has connections and I'm just a two-bit whore. He'll set me up."

Jake fell back on the hitchhiker's code. It did not matter that they had entered a new and yet to be defined relationship, he was still a hitchhiker, a visitor, a mere guest on a random highway. He could get off the ride any time he wanted and, as long as that was true, he was bound by the code not to interfere. He wanted to know everything but he was bound by the code not to ask any questions beyond: Where are you headed?

Ruby knew the code as well as anyone. All her life she felt as though she had lived in other people's homes, depending on the generosity of men. Her most recent vocation gave her a sense of freedom but, as it turned out, even that was an illusion. So she was acutely aware of Jake's dilemma. She believed they were bound together by forces that could not be denied but she wanted him to have free choice. She needed him to make that choice. She wanted him to sign on with his eyes wide open. She was a woman on the run, hunted by criminals and cops alike. The road ahead was uncertain and dangerous. He would have to balance the risks against the rewards – however sweet those rewards might be.

"Have you got a plan?" he asked.

Ruby smiled. It was as close to a commitment as she could reasonably expect.

"I'm working on it," she replied. "I made some calls. I know some people in Vegas who can fix me up: Fake ID, paint job, license plates, even a credit card. After that, I've got to put some miles between me and LA."

"That's a pretty good plan," said Jake.

Ruby wrapped her legs around him. "Thanks," she replied. "Are you in?"

Jake nodded and welcomed her embrace, dissolving at the scent of a woman in full bloom. It had been far too long since he had felt such divine pleasures.

"You should get some sleep," she said with a kiss. "We have to leave in a few hours."

His heart broke and his desire melted like wax in a Mississippi sun but he was an honorable man and he yielded to the need for sleep and the awakening that promised rebirth in a world of promise.

Under a bright, golden moon, they headed out over the southern branch of the Sierras. The path would take them through Death Valley to the city of neon lights where the gods of chance reign supreme. Ruby loved driving by moonlight and it seemed a good idea, under the circumstances, to take the road less traveled. It was a rough road but everything depended on reaching Vegas undetected.

Climbing a mountain road by the silver, moonlit waters of Lake Isabella, she thought of Isabel Allende's *House of the Spirits* and felt her passions rise. Her dark skinned hero by her side, she flipped on the radio and found an independent station on the FM band transitioning from jazz to nostalgic rock. Jake was moonstruck until she cranked it up as a Beatles medley came on, beginning with *I Want You* from *Abbey Road*. Ascending a steep grade near Walker Pass, she nearly lost control when the first chords of *Why don't we do it in the road?* from the White Album came roaring out of her speakers. She looked sideways at Jake and sensed that he was as aroused as she was.

She pulled off at the next lookout but before they could climb into the back seat an 18-wheeler came barreling by with its tires screeching and horns blaring. They watched in dumfounded awe and then listened as it crashed into a runaway truck ramp down the road.

A tall, thin Latino came jogging up the road, looking dazed and confused but otherwise unharmed.

"Are you kids alright?" he stammered.

"We're fine," replied Ruby.

"Wow!" he said. "Another second and you'd have been splattered. It's a miracle there was a turnout here."

They shared various expressions of relief and acknowledged that what had happened was beyond any reasoned explanation. A miracle? Ruby had no doubt and Jake had no denials. With the music pounding and the rising passion of the moment, neither Jake nor Ruby had seen or heard the approaching disaster. They didn't ask why he was driving an 18-wheeler down a narrow mountain road. They assumed it was the same reason Ruby had chosen this route: to avoid contact with the law.

Assured that everything was under control, they made their departure but not before Jake pointed out a marker by the side of the road. The white paint was yellowed and peeling, leading them to believe it was remnant of a former time. It read:

Mile 9.

Number nine, number nine, number nine…

SCENE 5: A LONG AND WINDING ROAD

FADE IN:

EXTERIOR DESERT HIGHWAY – SUNRISE

With Jake sleeping in the passenger seat, Ruby drives through Death Valley as the dark cloud of a sandstorm approaches.

The Beatles' GLASS ONION from the White Album plays in the foreground.

> *I told you about Strawberry Fields*
> *You know the place where nothing is real*
> *Well here's another place you can go*
> *Where everything flows.*
> *Looking through the bent backed tulips*
> *To see how the other half live*
> *Looking through a glass onion*

EXTERIOR SUBURBAN LAS VEGAS – DAY

A detective flashes his badge at the door of SISTER WOMAN, a friend of Ruby. She is small, dark skinned, with green eyes and flowing, Medusa-like hair.

EXTERIOR DEATH VALLEY – DAY

Jake and Ruby struggle against a powerful wind to secure the convertible top.

INTERIOR SISTER WOMAN'S HOUSE – DAY

The detective displays photographs, as he talks unheard: Ruby, Antonio, the boys. Sister Woman shakes her head and, then, shakes her head again.

INTERIOR RUBY'S CAR

As the sandstorm rages all around them, we see images from the tornado scene in *The Wizard of Oz*. A young girl runs into the arms of her father. Soldiers in a sandstorm fire at random as a chopper flounders above and crashes. A medicine man sits on a desert mountain, gazing at a sunset.

INTERIOR SISTER WOMAN'S HOUSE

Sister Woman follows the detective to the door. He lingers, handing her a card.

EXTERIOR SISTER WOMAN'S HOUSE FROM ABOVE

Ruby's Dodge pulls in the back of the house as the detective walks to his car.

INTERIOR SISTER WOMAN'S HOUSE

As Sister Woman closes the front door, Ruby knocks on

the back. Sister Woman rushes through the house, opens the door, and Ruby strikes a pose straight from the cover of Vogue.

....

Las Vegas is a city without time, born of desperate dreams and raised from a barren desert wasteland. It is a city that holds forth a promise of wealth and glory and delivers it to one in a million. To the 999,999 others it delivers a life of constant struggle and heartbreak. It is a city that calls out in neon: Give me your tired, your poor, your broken spirits yearning to break free. Above all, it is a city of delusions.

Ruby loved Las Vegas. In the diverse experience of her life, it was one of the few places that welcomed her without reservations. Ruby understood Las Vegas like she understood the silver phallus or the spotlight at a piano bar before karaoke. She understood the need and desire to hide dark secrets behind facades of splendor. For every nugget of gold in Vegas, there are a million of fools gold. For every genuine silver dollar, there are a billion wooden nickels. For every fine cut diamond, there are a trillion zirconium imposters. Just as the art of illusions transformed Vegas from a desert dream to a plaster and glitz paradise, Ruby hid her sorrow behind an inviting smile.

The sight and sounds of Las Vegas never failed to remind her of the county fair when she was a child of eight or nine. It was a simple time when her family maintained an illusion of happiness. It was not real. It was never real. For a while, however, it pleased them to believe they could be happy. Ruby reflected that her

mother had always believed in the miraculous power
of a smile. If you pretended you were happy and you
believed in the power, you could transform the reality
of your miserable life. Ruby's father – her stepfather
really but the only father Ruby had ever known – never
believed in the power but, for a while, he was willing to
pretend.

She remembered cotton candy, corn on the cob
slathered with creamy butter, and cows so big they
seemed like dinosaurs to a little girl with wide eyes.
She remembered the smell of barnyards, stale beer and
greasy burgers and pulled pork sandwiches. She
remembered carnies barking incomprehensible come-
ons. She remembered coin tosses, balloons and stuffed
pandas, unicorns and clapping monkeys. She
remembered feeling proud and special when her father
won the Wiley Coyote doll for her and only her.

They emerged from the desolate mountains, floated
through the hills and were now cruising down a desert
highway through Death Valley at sunrise. Jake sensed
her mood diving into darkness and felt the weight of
her silence but he had no concept of cause or remedy.
Despite the emerging sunlight, darkness was pervasive.
He was haunted by his own memories of youth when
the future was a promise and hope was his companion.
He remembered his grandfather taking him on
horseback to a high bluff overlooking the desert.

"Nothing in nature happens by accident," his
grandfather said. "Everything has a place and a
purpose. When brother hawk flies overhead, pay
attention. He has something to tell you. When the
snake crosses your path, turn around and walk back
the way you came. He is warning you that you are not

on the right path."

Ruby wiped away her silent tears and laughed when she saw that Jake noticed. "It's nothing, baby. Just memories."

They drove on in silence until they saw a billowing, dark cloud ahead, winding its way through a desert canyon like a mammoth serpent from an ancient tale of horror and foreboding.

"What is that?" asked Ruby.

"Shit," said Jake. He had seen such a sight before but never one so ominous. "Stop the car." Ruby slowed until they came to a stop. A massive sandstorm was rapidly approaching like the curse of a demon.

"We have two choices," said Jake. "We can go back the way we came or we can stay put and wait it out."

"Shit!" said Ruby. Her life was governed by a small set of golden rules, one of which was: Don't turn back. "Let's wait it out," she replied.

"Alright," said Jake. "Let's put up the top."

The wind howled like an angry preacher and the sand stung their skin and eyes as they struggled to secure the top of the convertible. By the time they were safely inside with the windows rolled up they could not see six inches in any direction. Ruby could have sworn she saw the Wicked Witch of the West riding her bicycle in the swirling, writhing storm, little Toto tucked in her wicker basket. She felt them being lifted off the earth and thought they might be swept away to the Land of Oz but feared there would be no Wizard or playful Munchkins. There would only be darkness and gloom. She felt a rush of anxiety, panicked and started to put Sadie in gear. If she was going down, she wanted to go down in motion, blazing a trail like James

Dean or Sarah Bernhardt.

Whatever she did, wherever she went, she did not want to die like Billie Holliday or Marilyn, lying in her bed, pumped full of poisons, sinking into the black hole of memories.

Jake gripped her arm and she remembered he was there. She was not alone. It was one thing to go out in flames. It was another to take someone else with you. For a million silver dollars or a promise of eternal bliss, she would never bring harm to Jake. She moved to him and felt his strength, his quiet courage, and his impregnable calm. He held her in his arms until the storm subsided and her sense of balance returned.

"Have you got a Plan B?" asked Jake.

"What do you mean, baby?"

Jake shook his head and looked her dead in the eyes. He was still the hitchhiker and mindful of his limitations but this was a powerful sign and he had to make her understand. It was not a game. It was real. It was happening. Why look to the signs if you are not willing to abide them?

"We're not supposed to go to Vegas," he said.

It hit Ruby like a blast of smoke and flame. She felt the life force drain from her body. She was instantly exhausted. She closed her eyes, leaned her head on the steering wheel and waited. When her energy returned it flooded her with rage. She flew out the door and cursed the gods, the fates and the muses. She cursed the desert and the blinding sand. She cursed the sun, the sky and the wisp of clouds hovering above. She cursed nine times, kicking up sand and pacing like a mad woman in a fit of insanity. Then she calmed down and climbed back in the car.

"You're right," she said. "The trouble is I don't have another plan. Everything depends on Vegas."

"Alright," said Jake. His mind was already racing ahead. He had the makings of a Plan B.

"I have no money," said Ruby. "I'm driving a car with a red neon sign that says: Arrest me! And I'm the most wanted woman in America! Hey, I'm a star! They'll make movies about me. Fuck! If I don't get to Vegas, baby, I don't have a chance."

"Alright," said Jake.

"Look, if you want to go back, I'll take you back. If you want to get off at the next town, fine. I understand. I get it. But I'm going to Vegas. I have no choice."

"It's alright," said Jake. "Just be careful."

"You're sticking with me?"

Jake nodded. Ruby gave a rebel yell, grabbed her man and painted his lips with gratitude. Then she popped Sadie Mae in gear and rolled down the road like a woman on a mission, like Sailor and Lula in *Wild at Heart*, like Jake and Elwood in *The Blues Brothers*. She burned through Death Valley, streaked over the mountains to the Nevada side and pulled up on a bluff overlooking the neon city.

"There she is," said Ruby. "Viva Las Vegas!"

She gave Jake a lingering wet kiss and proceeded with caution down the back roads to the home of her best friend in the suburbs. She parked in the alley, popped out of the car, knocked on the back door and struck a pose like the *Material Girl* in *Vogue*.

"Sister Woman!" she cried, as her friend grabbed her by the arm, yanked her inside and rushed to the front of her modest home, where she peeked out the window to make sure an unseen and unwanted visitor was long gone. He was.

Only moments before a Vegas detective had questioned Sister Woman, wanting to know the whereabouts of one Ruby Daulton and if she had been in contact. Meantime, Jake followed Ruby inside with the silence of a coyote on the prowl.

"Who the fuck is this?" cried Sister Woman. She drew her blinds and closed the back door before settling into her own prowl, a suburban prowl, a distinctly catlike prowl, back and forth in her living room. She was putting the voodoo telescope on him, cat against dog, tiger against wolf.

"You bring a strange man to my house?" she demanded.

"Relax," said Ruby. "This is Jake. I trust him like a brother."

"Yeah? Since when do you trust brothers?"

"Relax," Ruby repeated. "I trust him more than anyone I've known for the last three years. Hell, I trust him more than I do you!"

Sister Woman had to laugh at that and she let out her air.

"I'm Sister Woman," she said, extending her hand, which Jake took firmly.

"I'm Jake."

Everyone in Vegas had two or three names: one for the act, one for the second act, and one they kept to themselves for the family back home. Sister Woman was act two of Shirley Mann from Tupelo, Mississippi. She linked up with Ruby at a Vegas strip club and took refuge from an abusive boyfriend. She owed Ruby more than she knew and more than she wanted to owe anyone.

They sat down to cold beers and Sister Woman explained the layout like the point of an elaborate heist.

"Damn, girl, you're hotter than Beyonce! I hang up the phone, talking to Tony's boys, and a cop's at the front door, shooting the breeze and wanting to know what everybody wants to know: Where's Ruby?"

"You want to know what went down?" asked Ruby.

"I knew what happened when I first heard the news. The boys got frisky, Tony blew them away and pinned the rap on you."

Sister Woman lit up a cigarette and offered Ruby one.

"I don't have a lot of time," said Ruby, springing to her feet. "I need a credit card and twenty four hours."

"Got you covered," said Sister Woman.

She went into the bedroom and emerged with a shiny new credit card, bearing the name of Rhonda Whitney, and a fresh tag for her license plates.

"I would have got you the plates," she said, "but there wasn't enough time."

Ruby had tears in her eyes as she gave Sister Woman a warm embrace. It was more than she expected. They were sisters but in the life they were accustomed to living, sisters were one step removed from strangers or worse. Betrayal and payback were the lifeblood of their kind. They held on to each other a little longer than usual, knowing it was probably the last time they would come together.

"We're even now, girl," said Sister Woman.

"Twenty four hours," said Ruby. "Then we'll be even."

They left the way they came but Ruby lingered at the back door to look Sister Woman dead center in the eyes until she saw what she needed to see. Like so many hardened outlaws and criminals, more abused than abusing, there was tenderness beneath her cold exterior. There was true affection, even love, and Ruby was counting on it.

"Twenty four hours, baby."

"You got it, Ruby," said Sister Woman, her eyes welling with tears.

"I swear."

SCENE 6: ORPHEUS

FADE IN:

EXTERIOR SUBURBAN LAS VEGAS – ARIEL VIEW –
DAY

Ruby's baby blue Dodge convertible heads out of town,
Ruby driving with Jake in the passenger seat.

The Beatles' MARTHA, MY DEAR (White Album)
plays in the foreground.

> *Hold your head up you silly girl look what you've done*
> *When you find yourself in the thick of it*
> *Help yourself to a bit of what is all around you*

EXTERIOR DESERT HIGHWAY – DAY

Dilapidated vehicles abandoned alongside the road.
Close up of license plate "7FXY721" being removed.
Close up of license on Sadie Mae. Zoom out as Jake
and Ruby kick up dust heading back to town.

EXTERIOR LAS VEGAS – DAY

Close up of ATM cash withdrawal.

EXTERIOR LAS VEGAS – ARIEL VIEW – DAY

Ruby drives.

EXTERIOR CHOP SHOP OUTSKIRTS OF TOWN – DAY

Ruby exchanges cash with a tattooed man.

EXTERIOR CHOP SHOP – DAY

Ruby, Jake and the tattooed man play poker around a large wooden spool for chump change.

EXTERIOR CHOP SHOP – SUNSET

Ruby's Dodge freshly painted ruby red. CLOSE UP of a tear rolling down Ruby's face.

INTERIOR CASINO – NIGHT

Slow pan reveals Ruby at a poker table with a good stack of chips, Jake at the bar with a beer, and a couple of goons in cheap suits. They are MINNIE and SLIM, employees of Guido Lazerri.

When you find yourself in the thick of it
Help yourself to a bit of what is all around you

....

Ten years ago, a man named Giovanni Minolla, AKA Minnie, as much in reference to the legendary pool player, Minnesota Fats, as to his family surname, was a street vender selling sausages on the streets of Little Italy in Chicago.

Owing to a family recipe, Minnie's sausages were reputed to be the best in a city that prided itself on old style cuisine. It was his misfortune to be stationed at a street corner just across from Guido's Pizzeria.

As word spread, Minnie's sausages began to cut deeply into the pizzeria's business. Customers took to the habit of buying a sausage on the street and entering the pizzeria for its air conditioning and a cold brew.

The owner of the pizzeria was Guido Lazerri, a made man in a powerful crime syndicate. When Lazerri demanded an explanation for the decline in revenue, his manager, a beer bellied, self-promoting buffoon of a man, stammered and stuttered, afraid to inform the boss that the Lazerri recipe was second rate to that of a street vender. Guido had a reputation for volatility and not without reason.

A short, wiry busboy-dishwasher and general gopher, who went by the name of "Slim" for obvious reasons, whom everyone thought was mentally deficient because of his quiet nature and a spasmodic laugh that seemed to erupt without reason, stepped forward and told the truth.

Everyone in the restaurant froze in a slack-jawed, silent stare until a grim chuckle emerged from Guido's throat. He fired his manager on the spot and instructed Slim to invite Minnie in for a glass of Chianti and a couple of sausages.

Minnie became the new manager of Guido's

Pizzeria and Slim became his assistant. As Guido moved up the ranks in the organization, he brought Minnie and Slim with him.

They were profoundly grateful. In a business where loyalty is as rare as it is valued, loyalty was their primary asset. Whatever their shortcomings (and they had more than their share, one of which was not being able to recognize them), they could be counted on. They would give up their lives for Guido Lazerri. They would stare down the eyes of a dragon for the honor of their boss. They were groomed from the cradle the perfect lackeys and they were proud of it.

When Guido made the move west to take over a floundering gambling operation in Vegas, Minnie and Slim went with him.

Their current assignment was to track down a murderous, double-crossing bitch by the name of Ruby Daulton and they were hot on her tail. It was not a bad place to be.

Sitting on a barstool, sipping a beer, Jake was a little bored when he heard a sound, a low-pitched humming, that summoned his attention. He looked around at the symphony of flashing lights, clanging and jingling, and tired faces.

Ruby was doing well. She sat down at the poker table less than an hour ago and already she had a sizable stack of multicolored chips, whose meaning escaped him. She was in her element, a radiant jewel in a sea of common stone. He realized that the world would always be divided between life before Ruby and after Ruby. He would have been content to watch her play, to observe her inner joy, for as long as the moment endured but the humming entered his brain and beckoned like the siren song of ancient lore.

He looked around until he zeroed in on a poker machine across the room that seemed to emit an aura in red neon. He rose from the barstool and let the force of destiny pull him in. It was once in a lifetime and he savored the moment, like a mad scientist on the precipice of a universe-altering discovery.

Standing before a red neon machine, he reached into his pocket and pulled out a single silver dollar – the kind you get only at a Vegas casino. He plugged it in, punched the deal button and watched the adventure unfold in cinematic slow motion: Jack of Hearts, King of Hearts, Ace of Hearts, Ten of Hearts, Queen of Hearts.

A ruby red sea of hearts, the colors that turn seasoned gamblers green with envy and make believers of the most devout cynics. It was the ultimate high, an affirmation of all that was good and true, the homecoming of Ulysses, and proof of a divine being.

He smiled and stood in awe at the wonders of random chance. He believed neither in chance nor in the possibility of divine intervention and so his universe was torn asunder. Gravity was deconstructed and the earth beneath his feet became a sea of constant motion. He was no longer Jake Jones. He was above and beyond the man in his moccasins. He was someone else watching Jake Jones from a distance.

He was a little surprised that the machine did not spew a fountain of coins at his feet. Instead, a flashing red light and an alarm alerted all that a miracle had occurred on the casino floor. Another lucky winner! Another brash confirmation of the existence of god!

Elvis lives and Jim Morrison would have had it no other way. Here in the same casino where Tupac Shakur was shot down like a common thug, prayers were answered and dreams really did come true.

He felt a twinge of regret that Ruby was not there to share the moment. This was her turf, her kind of glory, and the dream that centered her existence. He looked in the direction of Ruby's poker table but his view was blocked, a crowd pushing in on him, and a beaming casino doll had just arrived speaking too rapidly for comprehension.

She counted out five big ones and chump change as a collective groan emerged from the onlookers. Jake smiled. It did not occur to him that the beauty of the experience could be mediated by the size of the wager. To him it was like a Hopper painting, a prime vintage wine, a ball player on a torrid hitting streak or the red rock towers of Monument Valley, but to the dispersing crowd it was a betrayal of the gambling gods, a cruel joke, and a testament to the folly of man.

He accepted their condolences and caught a glimpse of Ruby being hustled off the casino floor by a couple of greasy suits. She looked back and he saw panic etched on her tear-streaked face. Fate took its turn and something was horribly wrong.

By all measures, Ruby was an excellent poker player. She recognized the players and the marks at a glance. A mark could win a hand or two but only the players won in the long haul. It was rare to find a table without at least one player but two could easily share the winnings from a table full of marks.

Nobody's fool, Ruby knew the bogus credit card she

got from Sister Woman would not be good for long. She gave it a week at best. She needed hard currency and what better way to get it than at the Orpheus – a casino-hotel with connections to the mobster who placed her in jeopardy.

Having played less than an hour, she had collected over five grand in chips when she began looking for a graceful withdrawal. She glanced over to the bar and saw a stranger where Jake should have been. She looked around and her heart stopped, the earth tilted, and the force of gravity pulled her down. The familiar face of a grotesque fat man was staring at her with a crooked smile. An alarm and flashing lights signaled another lucky winner over at the poker machines as Ruby exchanged her chips for larger denominations, left the dealer a generous tip, and calmly rose from the table. If she could only make it to where the mindless swarm was gathering to witness the thrill of victory, maybe she could lose him.

It might have worked but the fat man's equally disgusting weasel of a partner was immediately at her side, grabbing her waist, pressing a gun to her back and guiding her to where the fat man waited.

"Sweet Ruby!" said the fat man.

"Hiya, boys," replied Ruby, not bothering to look them in the eyes.

It was not her first encounter with the Minnie and Slim act. She knew them from her drug running days, transferring contraband from LA and San Diego to party town Vegas. There was no point in starting up a conversation. The boys did what they were told. If they had orders to kill her, she was dead. If they had orders to turn her in, she was busted. If the boss wanted a word with her, she was headed up to the penthouse suite. They were moving toward the elevators in the hotel lobby so it looked like a personal interview with the big man at the top would be visiting her future. The worm turned along with a feeling in the pit of her gut.

She looked back once and caught a fleeting glimpse of a Royal Flush in Hearts. She wondered if it was the last hand she would ever see.

SCENE 7: PENTHOUSE PERVERSION

FADE IN:

INTERIOR HOTEL ELEVATOR – NIGHT

The Beatles' BLACKBIRD (White Album) plays in the foreground.

> *Blackbird singing in the dead of night*
> *Take these broken wings and learn to fly*
> *All your life*
> *You were only waiting for this moment to arrive*

CLOSE UP of Ruby, flanked by Minnie and Slim.   An elevator operator speaks into an intercom.

INTERIOR HOTEL LOBBY ELEVATOR ENCLAVE – NIGHT

Jake watches the elevator monitor rise to the 54th floor – the penthouse suite.

INTERIOR PENTHOUSE SUITE – NIGHT

A man in a stylish tailored suit looks out over the neon

Vegas strip. This is GUIDO LAZERRI, mob boss. The doors open and Ruby is escorted in, Minnie and Slim trailing behind.

Fade out BLACKBIRD:

You were only waiting for this moment to arrive

Fade in HELTER SKELTER:

When I get to the bottom I go back to the top…

INSERT MONTAGE – HELTER SKELTER

A whirlwind storm, overturned cars and boats, flying objects, naked dancers on a phallic pole, targeted missiles, explosions, charred bodies, Chernobyl, Exxon-Valdez, Bhopal, dead crows, quarantine bubbles and people in chemical suits. Dark images of masked, leathered bodies and faces intermixed with butchered meat and the pummeled faces of pugilists.

Fade out HELTER SKELTER.

Fade in WHILE MY GUITAR GENTLY WEEPS.

I don't know how you were diverted
You were perverted too
I don't know how you were inverted
No one alerted you

....

Despite the name, Guido Lazerri was not the typical Italian mobster cliché. He was definitely not Al Pacino in Scarface, Marlon Brando in The Godfather or James Gandolfini in The Sopranos. He more resembled a European businessman with enough charm, grace and taste to be welcomed in the most selective cultural circles. He was a smooth talker whose powers of persuasion transcended business and pleasure. He was accustomed to getting his way. He rarely had to ask.

As an illegitimate son of a prominent crime family patron, Guido was ideally positioned to advance in the ranks of the illicit empire. It was a time of great turmoil when the government, consumed in a war on terror, left criminal enterprise to its own policing. When the wheels of power turned one way, Guido was protected by his bloodline. When they turned the other way, he was shielded by his status as a bastard son.

He was a master strategist, a sound businessman, a smooth operator and a perverted prick. Before the advent of a pharmaceutical solution to the limp dick syndrome, Guido had a problem with his manhood. His Italian wife had a problem with the back of his hand. She never told anyone (perhaps she considered it her failing as a woman as her husband so often proclaimed) but when relatives from the old country came to visit, catching a glimpse of her bruises, it was made clear that if he ever laid hand on her again, he would not live to realize his ambitions.

Guido never laid hand on her again.

Thanks to the wonders of modern pharmacology, Guido became the man he always imagined himself to be. He inhabited strip clubs and hired a harem of prostitutes specializing in the dark arts of erotic perversion.

One of his favorite clubs was Shotgun Slim's and its owner, Antonio Menendez, became almost like a son to him – the son he could never produce, even with pharmacological assistance. Like nearly everyone who ever set foot in the place, Ruby Daulton was his favorite dancer but, out of respect for Tony, he never pushed it and Tony never offered.

The girls at the club talked about Guido Lazerri: He paid well but it took a week to wash the stench off their skin. No matter how kinky or masochistic a woman might be, Lazerri found a way to make her squirm.

Ruby knew enough about Guido to be petrified but she had a well-earned reputation in the biz as a tough girl and she would not give it up now. She would hold out for any prospect, however bleak, that she would survive the night.

When the boys escorted her through the door of his penthouse suite, she broke free and struck a pose like at third-rate actress at a third-rate theatre.

"Guido!" she intoned as she strutted across the room and planted a wet kiss and full body embrace on the man who held her life in his slimy hands.

Guido smiled and slapped her hard with the back of his hand. When she recovered, he slapped her again in the opposite direction. Ruby refused to fall. She took a couple of staggered steps back, wiped the blood from her lip and smiled back in defiance.

"So that's how you want to play, hey, baby?"

Guido loved everything about her: the way she talked, the way she walked, the way she smiled, the way she took a blow and came back for more. He had never seen her cry and suddenly that is what he desired more than anything else in his twisted universe. He wanted to break her defiant spirit like a wild Mustang. He turned to the boys, dumbfounded, and growled, "Get the fuck out!"

"Boss," said Slim, "she's got five grand in her pocket."

"That's my money," said Ruby.

"Where you're headed, darling, believe me, you won't be needing it."

Ruby felt the odds slipping as she reached into her pocket, extended her hand and dropped five grand in poker chips to the carpet. The boys scooped them up and headed out, Slim cackling under his labored breath, closing the door behind them.

"You want to know what happened?" asked Ruby.

"I already know what happened."

"Tony's little boys decided to give me a birthday party. They had it all planned."

"I already know…"

"Tony had an appointment. The party was supposed to end with me bending over my own couch, their loads up my…"

"Shut up, bitch!"

"Instead, Tony dropped by for a surprise visit."

"You liked it, baby!"

"Yeah, I liked it when he blasted their fucking heads off but I got out before he turned the gun on me."

"All women like it!"

"Fuck you, Guido!"

Guido was coming on to his pharmaceutical hard on. He was panting like a hungry dog at the gate of a bitch in heat. He wanted her so bad he was drooling on his tailored suit.

"You ran. Why didn't you call the police?"

"You know why."

"You're a liar. All women are liars!"

Hope on the wane, Ruby could no longer imagine a happy ending. She had been in desperate and kinky situations before. She could smell them. Some she walked into, others walked into her. Guido was kinkier than a homeless man's undershirt.

"Take your clothes off, baby."

"What?"

"You want something from me? You want me to make it all go away? You've got to give me a reason. You've got to give me what I need."

She was out of options. Time was the only one left. Guido loosened his belt and reached into his pants as Ruby began the slow dance of removing her clothing, just as she had done for Tony's boys. She was a singer at heart and her heart was singing the blues as if it was the last song she would ever sing. The guitar inside her soul gently wept.

"Turn around, bitch!"

He did not want to see her face just yet, her eyes, the buildup to tears running down her cheeks. He did not want to see her passion, her hatred, her pity or the depth of her humanity. He wanted a plaything, a doll, a warm, bleeding piece of flesh into which he could insert his proof of manhood.

Ruby let the last piece of clothing, her black silk panties, drop to the floor and tried not to gag as she felt Guido's breath on her neck, his hand on her ass, his sweaty fingers sliding up and down. She tried to imagine cotton candy at the County Fair.

There was a loud crash outside the door. Ruby

spun and caught Guido off guard. She kicked as hard as she could, as if the life of her child depended on it, connecting square between his legs, and watched him crumble to the plush white carpet.

Jake came crashing through the door, gun in hand, and delivered a blow to Guido's head that sent him to another universe where pain and suffering would be his loyal attendants, where the abuser became the abused.

Ruby embraced her hero and painted his face with a thousand kisses, tears streaming from her eyes and visions of horror worse than death fading from her mind.

Life was a strange and brutal place and yet there were men like Jake Jones, women like Ruby Dalton, who proved that it was not all bad. There was kindness, courage, dignity and beauty. And there was hope. There was still hope.

Ruby pulled on her clothing as quickly as she could and the two of them rushed out into the hall, past a cursing Minnie and Slim, hogtied on their slimy bellies, past an unconscious and tied elevator attendant, his body obstructing the elevator door.

They exited on the second floor and continued their escape by the stairwell. It was Helter Skelter and they were on the move. As long as they could keep moving, never stopping, never looking back, Ruby felt they would be all right.

They sprang into a warm and glorious Las Vegas night. It was still a magical city, a city where dreams could still come true, a city where hope was alive until the last bet was wagered, and a city where a single silver dollar could reveal the most precious and rare treasure: a royal flush in ruby red hearts. They were alive and kicking and on this particular night, with the neon lights warming the air around them, hustling through swarms of wide-eyed tourists, it was all that mattered.

SCENE 8: NIGHT OF THE WORM

FADE IN:

EXTERIOR DESERT HIGHWAY – NIGHT

Ruby and Jake drive beneath a starlit sky. Pools of car light shine on a two-lane highway, heading east in a sea of sand, tumbleweed and mountains of naked stone.

The Beatles' BLACKBIRD plays in the foreground.

> *Blackbird singing in the dead of night*
> *Take these sunken eyes and learn to see*
> *All your life*
> *You were only waiting*
> *For this moment to be free*

Fade out BLACKBIRD.

Fade in HELTER SKELTER.

> *When I get to the bottom I go back to the top…*

INTERIOR LAZERRI'S PENTHOUSE SUITE – NIGHT

Minnie, Slim and a security guard stand facing an

enraged Guido Lazerri, his shirt undone, his fly open and his engorged prick exposed.

Do you don't you want me to love you?

Guido holds a gun to Minnie's head and holds it as Minnie breaks down and cries.

Well you may be a lover but you aint no dancer

Guido adjusts his pants, places the gun on his desk and makes a phone call.

Now Helter Skelter, Helter Skelter...

....

Their minds flew across the barren wasteland, forgotten lands of no tomorrows, where Mother Nature's daughter remains unspoiled, unused, untapped, naked in her thirst and virgin in her desire. Particles of light danced before their eyes, painting pictures in the heart, transforming all it graces into images of living art.

In another part of the world, men and women, children and newborn babies were living with the constant, pounding drumbeat of war. Bombings, night raids, torture, rape, suffocating gas, electro-shock, burying the dead, nursing the wounded, and the ever present wailing of mothers in mourning.

Here in America, we were only beginning to awaken to the nightmare we unleashed upon the world. Our fortune squandered, our freedom shackled, our lives of quiet desperation, sifting through the sands of time for something lost or something found to renew the dream.

"How did you do that?" asked Ruby.

Jake had disarmed three grown men without killing or being killed, without harming or being harmed, without even firing a shot. Like a native superman, he answered her hour of need when he could have easily put out his thumb and taken the next ride.

"I'm a ghost," said Jake. His mind still soaring on desert winds high above them, breathing in the land of his forbearers, he spoke the truth but without conscious thought. "Kachina magic," he added.

Ruby laughed but the pain of her swollen face choked her spirit. She was a broken girl on a road to nowhere. She had no future and her past was cut off like a severed limb. Vegas was fading in the rearview mirror, a neon dream turned night horror. Vegas was her town, the only place on earth that breathed life into her tired, broken soul. Now she realized she could never go back. Vegas used to be her town. Now she was homeless.

"Asshole," she muttered through her tears.

Jake came to attention and Ruby smiled. "Not you, baby. I was just thinking of Tony and that worm Guido. The people we learn to trust because we're on the same side, we go to the same joints, know the same friends, speak the same lingo. People with power. The rest of us are just peons, chumps, idiots."

"People with dreams," replied Jake. "People with stars in their eyes."

Ruby ran through it a few times before deciding she

liked it.

"Thanks, baby," she said. "People with stars in their eyes."

She drove on into the endless night, thinking about how strange life could be, how difficult it was to hold on to the belief that everything had a purpose and that somehow everything would turn out for the best. She desperately needed to hold on to that dream no matter how unlikely it seemed, no matter how often life's twists and turns beat her down like an ill-mannered dog. She needed to believe or she would fade away. Now more than ever she needed to be strong.

She linked up with the asshole because he offered her a life that was just a little better than the one she had – or so she thought at the time. It was a way of life, inching along, clawing and scratching, climbing up the endless stairway one step at a time. A fool's game never delivered what it promised. She thought she could handle it and she had until fate played its hand.

The life she had lived before Tony was not all that bad: a stripper/dancer/singer, sleeping by day, working by night, consuming drugs instead of food, trying like hell to find the door to Hollywood success just like a hundred thousand other pretty girls just like her. Well, they were not exactly like her. Ruby could sing like Billie Holliday. She could act like a young and fearless Norma Jean, she could dance like Gwen Verdon in a Bob Fosse dream, but all they saw and all they wanted to see was flesh.

Ruby gave them what they wanted but they always wanted more. All that crap about casting couches: Ruby wished it was that easy. In her experience, sleeping with a director or producer was the surest way to put you outside the Hollywood circle. It might work if you were already inside but if you were outside looking in it kept you there. The scumbags didn't want to be reminded of the scumbags they really were.

She sighed and imagined translucent blue light surrounding her, emanating from the core of her being. She breathed in the cool dry air and found herself floating on a sea of green waves to a paradise of tropical ease. She glanced at the golden bronze face of the man beside her and wondered how long it would be before he asked who was who and what was what. As he floated in his own wonderland of flight, she realized he never would. He was a different kind of man, a kind she had never before encountered, the kind that would always be a mystery.

Ruby loved mysteries.

She felt the attraction of a Sleepy Time Motel before it came into view. She pulled off the highway onto the gravel lot and took note of a run down bar across the street.

"I need a drink," she said.

Jake smiled, stealing a moment of reorientation as she parked in the back. They booked cabin number nine and crossed the street, walking past an old Desoto and a couple of Harley Davidson's. When their eyes adjusted to the dim lighting, they made out two bikers at the bar, half watching a baseball game on TV, a cowboy bartender, and a couple of Navaho men at a corner table.

All eyes zeroed in on Ruby's sensual grace. They hardly seemed to notice her bruised and battered face as she excused herself to the restroom with a wink and smile.

"What are we drinking?" she said in parting.

Jake took a quick account of the situation, the circumstance, the alignment of planets and the pull of gravity.

"Dos Gusanos," he said.

Ruby smiled again and blew a kiss over her shoulder. It was the night of the worm. So be it. The last time she ate the worm she woke up on an unmarked grave in a pauper cemetery somewhere outside of Hornitos in the California foothills. She vaguely remembered a couple of Chicanos who went by the names of Joaquin and Three Fingered Jack. That was the last recollection she had. The worm was always good for erasing memories. What could be better for a couple of outlaws on the run?

The first time Jake ate the worm he was riding a peyote vision, trading tales with Don Juan on a private tour of Ixtlan, sharing laughter and an appreciation of the lucidity of life. It was when Jake learned to fly. The last time he ate the worm he almost jumped off the edge of Grand Canyon.

The bartender poured a couple of shots with a couple of beer chasers and Jake made two trips to a table at the front of the bar, next to the door. Worm or no worm, it was the kind of place that called for a quick exit if the worm turned the wrong way. He returned to the bar, dropped a large denomination and the bartender handed over the bottle – con gusanos.

It was half full or half empty and the evening was filled with possibilities.

When Ruby made a stunning re-entrance, the bikers swiveled on their bar stools and openly drooled as she strutted to their table, grabbed a shot and toasted, "The

Worm!"

Jake took note of the bigger of the two bikers, the kind who went by "Tiny" in high school, never graduated from the football field, and later was christened "Bear" or "Moose" in a supreme insult to the animal kingdom. Trouble was brewing in the space behind his tarnished, yellow eyes and he made no effort to hide it.

One eye on Ruby and one on Jake, he hitched his jeans and walked to the old jukebox, plopped in a few quarters and pecked out a three-digit number he knew by rote. Everyone in the house had heard this tune before.

I've been a fool for every fallen angel
That ever asked me once or asked me nice
But not like the fool I was for you dear
When I walked up to you and broke the ice

He stood before them, leather and blue jeans, hands behind the back, like a teen at his first social, shuffling his boots and rattling his chains.

"Wanna dance?"

Ruby examined the back of his skull and went for the bottle.

"Sorry, Cowboy, I'm all danced out. Let's go, Jake."

Cowboy shuffled his boots to let Ruby by and planted himself in Jake's path.

"That's fine, little lady. Some women like half-breeds who slap them around."

Jake went for the balls with his knee, followed by a stiff left and pushed him back with a kick to the chest. He motioned Ruby to stand back, placed himself by a solid brick wall, lowered his center of gravity and braced. Cowboy charged him like a rabid bull, snorting and heaving as he pounded across the wooden floor.

Jake grabbed Cowboy's clenched fists, absorbed the blow against the wall and let his body serve as conduit, channeling the beast's aggressive force into a well-placed knee at the center of his personality disorder. The monster was dead and all that remained was a groaning mass of flesh on the floor, holding his hands like they were useless appendages.

It happened so fast the biker's partner was still on his stool.

"Kachina magic!" announced Ruby. "Don't mess with it."

The Navahos at the corner table smiled and glared at the cowboy still standing.

Jake and Ruby walked out, arm in arm, like Frankie and Johnny at the height of their madness, an undeniable force, a bullet train to the heart of darkness, untouchable, invincible and true. Their legend would follow wherever they went and stories would be told to grandchildren.

As they walked across the street to cabin number nine, Ruby took a swig and passed the bottle. It felt like a beginning, a bond consummated in blood, tears and the liquid language of eternal love. Ruby felt alive and Jake had no desire to be anywhere but at Ruby's side. It did not matter that they came from different worlds. Nothing mattered but the moment and the understanding that all of life on earth was encapsulated in a single particle of time. Divinity or chance, a hand reached out of the great mystery to push two particles together and together they would remain until divinity or chance broke them apart.

Tonight they would drink the worm!

They sat on their king sized double bed, feasting on vending cuisine, smoking and drinking until the worm settled and their souls began to dance.

Sweet serenade of sensual rapture, wet reptilian curls, a dance of moonlight on crystal waterfalls, the magnetic pull of black hole gravity on the salted sea of earthly desire. Paralytic enchantment, suspension of time, abdication of the laws of physics, giving without will, receiving without wonder, Jake and Ruby danced to the music of life in the swirling, twisting, writhing center of all creation.

If this was not love, then it had no name and love was filled with envy.

Captured by Ruby's glistening white body, her movement the poetry of truth, admiring Jake's golden grace, his heaving strength, swimming in each other's ponds of devotion, Jake believed in love and Ruby believed in destiny.

Blackbird singing in the dead of night
Take these broken wings and learn to fly
All your life
You were only waiting
For this moment to arise

SCENE 9: CASH ON THE LAMB

FADE IN:

EXTERIOR DESERT – SUNRISE

The Beatles' I'M SO TIRED plays in the foreground.

> *I'm so tired I don't know what to do*
> *I'm so tired my mind is set on you*
> *I wonder should I call you*
> *But I know what you'd do*

EXTERIOR MOTEL ROOM – DAY

The curtains open, revealing a naked Ruby greeting the morning.

INTERIOR SEEDY BAR – NIGHT

Close up of a customer watching a naked dancer, one hand rubbing his crotch.

Fade out I'M SO TIRED. Fade in HAPPINESS IS A WARM GUN.

She's well acquainted with the touch of the velvet hand
Like a lizard on a windowpane
The man in the crowd with the multicolored mirrors
On his hobnail boots
Lying with his eyes while his hands are busy working
overtime

INTERIOR MOTEL ROOM – NIGHT

JAKE sleeps.

Fade out HAPPINESS. Fade in I'M SO TIRED.

You know I can't sleep, I can't stop my brain
You know it's three weeks, I'm going insane
You know I'd give you everything I've got
For a little peace of mind

JAKE awakens with a start.

Fade out I'M SO TIRED. Resume HAPPINESS.

I need a fix 'cause I'm going down
Down to the bits that I left uptown
I need a fix 'cause I'm going down

....

It was hot that summer. Relentlessly hot. A rising temperature was already creeping into the early morning hours, slipping through the cracks and crevices, warning all inhabitants to take shelter before the midday sun pounded them into submission. Normal people heeded the warning, waiting out the days in shaded, air-conditioned rooms or seeking refuge in chlorine filled pools of liquid relief. Others had pressing business that could not wait for a change in the weather.

Ruby was awakened by the adventure in her heart. She was alive! Kick up your heels, pedal to the metal, keep on rockin' in the free world alive!

Naked as a cloudless day, she pulled opened the curtains and breathed in the spirit of mystery, the unspeakable joy of living, the randomness of life on the run, cheap motels, gravel parking lots, the smell of asphalt, gas and oil, greasy roadside diners and highway rest stops where hustlers and low lifers always gathered.

Damn, it doesn't get any better than this!

Ever since she was a small child, she loved the view from a car seat. She loved the sensation of motion, the liquidity of time, the flow of transport, the excitement of new places, new faces, new conversations, new rules of engagement, new accents, new manners of speech, new cultures and new expectations. Ruby loved the rhythm of the road, itself, the staccato dotted line, the rolling wires and telephone lines, the sudden eruption of city lights and the gradual resumption of barren wastelands and the great expanse.

She loved looking at life framed in a windshield, history in a rearview mirror.

She was jazzed by the adrenalin rush of not knowing what the day would bring: another crisis, another mind numbing brush with death or worse, another Kachina rescue bringing her back from the brink of another disaster.

It was time to get a move on. Lay down some miles

between them and their pursuers but a glance at her still sleeping lover left her sighing. He was so beautiful in his dream state, so peaceful and open. She could not wake him. She could not bring him back from where he was just now.

She had a plan. Head south, cross the border at Nogales and kiss the stars and stripes forever goodbye. A long weekend in Tampico, sipping Margaritas, whispering sweet temptations beneath the sound of mariachi bands until the worm settled and the trail cooled to a tepid lull. Then they would amble up the Gulf Coast to New Orleans, the Big Easy, the Crescent City, the soul of American jazz and the heartbeat of a continent, where Ruby could begin life anew. It was a place she had dreamed of where they welcomed and appreciated a woman of her special talents.

It was a decent plan and, better yet, it just might work but it all depended on a little cash. The credit cards from Vegas were stone dead, a ticket straight to jail or another round with Guido, Tony and the boys. She shredded them and scattered the remains across a hundred miles of desert.

Ruby knew how to raise cash but she didn't know if Jake could hang with it. Overcome by her enthusiasm, she rolled to the bed and kissed his eyes and lips awake as gently as she knew how.

His eyes rolled and struggled for the light that would lead to the bridge that would cross the divide between his dream and the world where Ruby was queen. He looked like the lone survivor of an airline crash, hair tangled in an Einstein maze, eyes bulging and streaked with red, blue highways on a crumpled map.

"Ruby," he said through layers of fog, "I have to sleep."

His eyes rolled back and Ruby sensed panic slipping up her spine. He looked like a dozen shades of death. He seemed apart from the world, alien to planetary life. Was he sick? She laid her hand on his forehead: a little warm, a little clammy, nothing alarming.

"I'm fine," he mumbled beneath the veil. "I just need...sleep."

He wanted to say she should go on without him but he was already far away, a stranger in a distant land, removed in both time and space. Where he was headed he did not know and Ruby could not follow.

"It's alright, baby," she said, placing a gentle kiss on his forehead. "Sleep."

He wanted to tell her it was not the first time. It began when he was a child, a water born sickness his mother had said. Others said it was a curse born of an evil white man's presence on the night of his birth. Still others, spirit guides and prophets, said it was a gift like that of Crazy Horse and Wavoka. It was bridge to the Overworld where the mysteries of the universe unfolded and pearls of wisdom could be gathered. As he grew into a man, the occurrence was sporadic and infrequent but it arrived without warning and hit like a hammer between the temples. He would sleep for at least eighteen hours. There were times when he was unconscious for three days.

Down. Ruby was crashing. She gazed at Jake's fluttering eyeballs beneath closed lids and she felt herself spiraling downward. All the gods and goddesses that looked over her shoulder in times of trouble had vanished like shadows in light. Sleeping at the bottom of a dark lagoon.

She paced the room, pulled at her hair, and cried when the only word to emerge from Jake's lower depths was: Dance.

She went to him, placed her tears upon his lips, and pleaded: "What was that, baby? You want me to dance?"

He was gone. Not even a glimmer. She felt a surge of anger immediately choked back by a torrent of tears. It was not time to leave her man. Fate could be a cruel master but at this time and place it was insufferable. She had to think.

She recovered as quickly as she crumbled. There was no reason why she couldn't make this work. Dance. She would let him sleep as long as it took. She would drive to Phoenix, find a club and raise enough cash for the journey ahead. Dance.

She went through Jake's pockets, pulled out his wallet and was surprised to find over three hundred cash. She took a hundred as a loan, fixed herself up in the bathroom mirror and kissed her sleeping lover goodbye.

On her way out, she paid the clerk for another night and hit the road.

"Terrible," said the heavily accented Asian Indian behind a plexiglas barrier.

"What's that?" said Ruby.

"The war," he replied. "There will be no end."

"Yeah," said Ruby. "Terrible."

She hadn't thought about the war in weeks and she felt a little guilty. No matter how bad things were and no matter how bad they would get, it could be worse.

She could be the mother of a child in Fallujah or some forsaken city under siege by foreign soldiers. She shook it off and went her way. With all the shit that was happening there was only so much she could take in and endure. She cleared her mind and drove down the highway in a haze, letting the heat wash over her like a blast of molten lava.

Phoenix was a strange town, a rightwing fundamentalist town. Like all fundamentalist towns, there was money to be made on the dark side. The uptight, Bible quoting, church-going throng always managed to populate the gin joints and strip clubs on the outskirts and in the underbelly of town.

Ruby bought a wispy blue chiffon outfit at a Salvation Army outlet and staked out a two-story brick club with a red neon "Bimbo's" sign on its veneer. After a few hours, she was reasonably sure they were not connected to the Lazerri clan. She went in to apply for a slot in the evening rotation.

One look and the bald fat man who ran the joint knew she was a winner. She used the name Sadie Mae, flashed her fake ID and offered to work under the table, tips only, cash on the line. He welcomed her to "the family" with a fat man belly laugh and a handshake, the other hand rubbing his crotch.

When Ruby took the stage, she was the prized creation of another world, a world where movement was slow and sensual, where dance was second nature. She floated over the floor, painting circles with her grace, coiling around the metal phallus like a snake. The easy elegance with which she bared her private beauty released all sense of shame and left them rich with envy, comfortable in their collective depravity, shaking with raw desire, and alive with pounding sweat. She gave them sweet dreams of divine pleasure and accepted their generosity with a smile.

Four hundred in the first set and she was only getting started. The city that rose from a desert wasteland never saw a bird like Ruby and no one who witnessed her exquisite dance would ever forget. Every man, from the pastor to the chief of police, would see Ruby in his dreams and in the eyes of his wife or lover ever after.

Another set and Ruby left with over a grand and an invitation from the fat man to return whenever she pleased. She brushed off three or four sleazy, sweaty propositions and drove home to her still sleeping prince.

Jake came to only long enough for a drink of water and half an explanation of his disorder. It was enough for Ruby. He told her she could go on without him and maybe she should but Ruby had no intention of leaving this place without him. She had a plan and she was sticking to it.

Another night, another performance, another grand and Ruby was feeling good, top of the world and ready to celebrate.

Jake awakened with a start, sat up on the motel bed, and waited for his eyes to find vision in the waking world. He found a note on the table: "Gone to work. Be home late. Love, Ruby." There was an envelope with nine hundred dollars in it and a matchbook from a club called "Bimbo's" in Phoenix. He threw some water on his face, got dressed, walked out to the highway and stuck out his thumb.

When a cute blonde with cropped hair, blue eyes and a sleek body reminiscent of Lula in *Wild at Heart* invited Ruby for a couple of drinks at an after-hours club, she thought "no" but said "Sure." When Laura's boyfriend met them outside, she thought "trouble" but she went along. When Laura suggested that they ride together, she thought "bad idea" but she found herself in the shotgun position in the cab of an old Ford pickup.

"It could be worse," she thought. She could be trapped between them. "Nothing's going to happen," she told herself.

Ruby believed in the phenomenon known as a self-fulfilling prophecy and fear, in her philosophy, was an invitation to danger but she could not ignore the knot that was tightening in the pit of her gut.

She let it go when, to her relief, they arrived at a secluded joint called The Salty Dog in a dark, run-down city landscape of two-story brick buildings. She relaxed when they started knocking down margaritas over Roy Orbison ballads in a red leather booth.

On the third margarita, Laura placed her hand delicately on Ruby's thigh and met no resistance. Ruby's head was spinning, her spirit swimming in swirling waves of hot liquid. She was beyond control, hearing something about three-way sex as her escorts held her arms and guided her out into the street.

"Jake!" she said, propped between Laura and her leather lover. "How did you find me?"

"A friend of yours overheard a conversation at Bimbo's," he replied. "Time to go home."

"Hey," said Laura with a seductive smile, "we were thinking of taking it to our place. You're welcome to join us."

"I don't think so," said Jake, pulling Ruby from their reluctant grip and leaning her against a parked car.

Leather made a move for a gun parked in the small of his back but Jake flashed his hunting knife in the glimmering moonlight.

"You move that hand another quarter inch, you're as dead as Custer at the Greasy Grass," said Jake.

Leather raised his hands as Laura said, "Hey, nothing personal. It's just business."

Jake took the gun, emptied it, and tossed it down the road.

On the ride back to the motel, Ruby muttered "Kachina magic" before she slipped into the nether land of drug-inspired dreams.

EXTERIOR ARIEL VIEW – NIGHT

A car riding down a lonesome highway.

The Beatles' HAPPINESS plays in the foreground.

> *Mother Superior jump the gun*
> *Mother Superior jump the gun*
> *Happiness is a warm gun*
> *Bang Bang Shoot Shoot*

Fade HAPPINESS and resume I'M SO TIRED.

> *I'm so tired I haven't slept a wink*
> *I'm so tired my mind is on the blink*

FADE OUT.

SCENE 10: METAMORPHOSIS

FADE IN:

EXTERIOR DESERT HIGHWAY – ARIEL VIEW –
NIGHT

Ruby and Jake drive down a two-lane highway, top
down, hair flying in the wind.

We hear the Beatles' OB-LA-DI, OB-LA-DA in the
foreground.

> Obladi oblada life goes on bra
> Lala how the life goes on

Fade in GLASS ONION over. Fade OB-LA-DI to
background.

> I told you about strawberry fields
> You know the place where nothing is real
> Well here's another place you can go

CLOSE UP of a rabbit, big brown eyes in the light. It
dashes across the road. Ruby slams on the brakes but
cannot avoid hitting it. Jake and Ruby stand over the

corpse in a pool of light.

Fade in OB-LA-DI over.   Fade GLASS ONION to background.

EXTERIOR DESERT HIGHWAY – NIGHT

CLOSE UP of Jake driving and Ruby staring blankly into the night.

Fade in GLASS ONION. Fade out OB-LA-DI.

> *Standing on the cast iron shore – yeah*
> *Lady Madonna trying to make ends meet – yeah*
> *Looking through a glass onion.*
> *Oh yeah oh yeah oh yeah*

....

A balancing act on the edge of obscurity, one small step for man, one giant leap for evolution, a high wire balance on Dante's dilemma, a gateway to beyond the beyond, the precipice of absolute abandon, a black hole of extermination, metamorphosis and rebirth.

Dreams are the other side of finite.

Ruby awakened in the dark of night, jumped out of bed and announced, "Get dressed, lover. There's a full moon rising on a highway of dreams and we've got three hundred miles of asphalt to lay!"

Jake was ready. He would not need sleep for another twenty-four hours minimum. He joined her in the shower and was dressed and waiting by the time she emerged in full black-leather beauty: black leather pants and jacket, ankle high boots with metal tips and one-inch spikes, with a ruby red silk blouse tied to expose her slender white midsection. She shook the water out of her hair and completed a portrait in the mirror with black teardrop shades.

"Who loves you, darling?" she purred.

"I do," replied Jake in the confines of his mind.

She was a reptile, he thought, shedding her skin like others changed underwear. She was the star of her own movie and he liked it that way. Jake was not a man who coveted attention. He preferred to watch from the edge until the time was ripe to act.

"I've got a fistful of dollars and a solid plan," she announced. "We head south, cross the border at Nogales, two weeks of Margaritas to let the heat subside, then we make a beeline to New Orleans. How does that sound?"

Jake was stunned. It was as good a plan as any and Ruby had every right to follow her own instincts. The problem was he could not go south. He sat down on the bed and let the river wash over him.

Ruby was shaken. She was not a woman to second-guess her decisions but Jake was her guardian spirit, her guide and protector. If Jake was not on board it was a problem. They were a team, joined at the hip for the length of the dance. Surely by now he understood. She cocked her head and thought twice. Maybe she was being presumptuous. Maybe saving her life twice in a span of days was enough for any man. She understood the rules. She was the driver and he was the ride. But after all that had happened the least she could do was listen to him.

"What is it, baby?"

"I can't go south," he said. "In the other world, I traveled the four directions. I saw a great upheaval to the west, battle lines and an army of protest. I saw a great silence to the north, as if waiting, biding time. To the east, I saw masks of deception, people in power talking in rhymes and riddles, smoke and mirrors. To the south, I saw death, walking corpses, the cries of women and children.

"It is the one way I can't go. It isn't my time to die."

Ruby sat beside him on the bed and let the river wash over them both. She believed him as a child believes her mother, as a believer believes the prophet. She would find another way. She grabbed a newspaper, spread it on the floor, marked the four directions, and spun a bottle at its center. North, said destiny. North.

"North?" questioned Ruby. "What's north?"

"The Canyon," answered Jake.

The moon was nearing its fullness, casting an eerie luminescence over the desert landscape. Jake knew this land well. It was the land of his people, home of his ancestors, hunting grounds of the Apache, Arapaho, Navaho, Hopi and Paiute.

He had wandered this land for as long as he could walk and Grand Canyon was the solar plexus of it all. The offspring of Pluto's seed and Persephone's fall, it was a door to the other side of light, the dark matter of scientific wonder. It made small children of giant men. It was a place of intense power, where the heartbeat of the continent could clearly be heard.

No one could look into the Grand without sensing the majesty of Mother Earth.

Jake knew the canyon from the eyes of the crow to

the trails of the wild burros. He knew where the wind currents ran, as faithfully as the Colorado River below, and where an unsuspecting off-the-path tourist could be swept into the bottomless chasm.

Music blaring from the radio, the wind running through them like a first winter's morning, they kicked up their heels and drove as if it was the road to nowhere – no worries, no cares, no remorse or guilt. None of the self-inflicted wounds we embrace to make us feel as if we are alive. They needed no more than the air in their lungs and the spirit of the open sky to know that the pulse of life pounded within them like a dozen metal drums in Jackson Square. It was all they could do not to pull over and make love on the side of the road.

The Canyon was pulling them forward, singing an impetuous song, sending out a magnetic ray of life, as bright as destiny, itself.

"Canyon is number nine," said Ruby.

The canyon was the pull of infinite death and only the brave at heart could receive its blessing. Only those who could stand on the precipice and stare into its depths, its soul of darkness, its mad temptation, could behold its sacred light.

The Canyon is number nine.

"Shit!" said Ruby with a glance at the flashing light streaking over them like laser daggers. "Fucking cops," she announced.

Too late to run and nowhere to go, she pulled over and assumed the posture: a helpless woman, sexy beyond dreams but clueless beyond credibility. The officer remained in his car, running the plates and talking to an unseen force.

"Shit," said Ruby, "Guido tipped them off. I should have killed the bastard!"

Jake glanced over his shoulder and remained perfectly still, perfectly calm. Ruby had her way of dealing with the law. Jake had his.

"Good evening, officer," Ruby purred.

"License and registration," said the officer, stealing a glance at Ruby's endowment and keeping an eye on Jake for any signs of danger.

"Is this your vehicle, m'am?" he asked, staring at her phony license.

"Why, yes, officer. Why?"

"Just doing my job, Miss…Whitney."

"Of course, officer."

"Headed for the Canyon, are you?"

"Yes we are, officer."

"That's fine, Miss Whitney, just slow it down and have a nice day."

Arizona's finest got back in his cruiser, turned around, and drove back the way he came. Something was rotten. It was not how the script read.

Jake looked at Ruby. Ruby stared into the rearview mirror.

"That's fucked up," said Ruby.

"Let's go," said Jake.

The Canyon beckoned. They drove on, Jake a blank slate, impenetrable, while Ruby's mind churned like the internal workings of an industrial symphony. Why wasn't she behind bars? Who tipped them off? Was it someone in LA, someone in Vegas? Who wanted her? Was it Tony or Guido or both? How did they track her? Was it someone in Phoenix? She wasn't speeding. How did they know where to find her?

She would later learn, in a short phone conversation, that she was off the hook. They were railroading someone else. Tony found another stooge. He wanted to deal with Ruby himself. For now, it was a mystery.

There was only one way into the Canyon and one way out. She drove on as if driving itself would reveal the key that would release her. One way in and one way out. Not even Jake could save her this time. Or could he? This was Jake's choice and he was determined to go to the Canyon. Every instinct told her they were on the wrong course. They should turn around and get the hell out. Even then there was no assurance that Lazerri's boys wouldn't be waiting for them. She wondered if it wasn't yet another test of faith. This time it was her faith in the man who sat beside her.

They pulled up to the gate and drove straight through. No one from the park was there to take their money or check their ID's. Jake directed her to an overnight parking lot.

"Are you worried?" he asked.

"No, baby," replied Ruby. "I'm all out of worry. Just point me to the edge and I'll follow you over."

"You'd do it," smiled Jake.

"Baby," replied Ruby, "I'd follow you anywhere."

Jake looked at her as if he had never seen her before, as if he had never held her in his arms and tasted her lips, as if he had never been lost in the electrical storm their bodies unleashed on an undeserving world, as if he had never known her most singular mystery.

"I believe you would," he said.

Ruby felt warm and undiscovered. If this was not

love, it would do. If she never knew love again, it would do. If nothing else, in a life filled with sorrow and misfortune it would serve to answer the mystery of love. What more could she ask of him?

Jake pulled a small flask from his pack and Ruby followed him down to a place by the ledge, at the edge of the world by the canyon of infinite awe.

"Wow!" said Ruby. She was a singer, a dancer, not a poet. She stood before the most powerful signature of a divine force any man or any woman could ever witness and all she could think to say was "Wow!"

They sat in the light of a three quarter moon and watched the canyon transform. Jake drank from the flask and passed it to Ruby. It was mescal, a medicinal from the desert tribes that aided the seer's vision, bringing a blessing of second sight. They watched the river below bulge and shrivel as the canyon inhabitants struggled and thrived, indifferent to the external world. Clouds seemed to spring from her bowels, growing and spreading until it reached the ledge below their feet. They saw a thousand pairs of eyes watching them as they watched the canyon.

The dark philosopher said: If you gaze into the abyss too long, the abyss will gaze into you. The philosopher of light said: If you gaze into the mystery it will enter your soul and you will never be alone.

The clouds began their retreat with the first light of day and the sounds of awakening canyon life emerged. They rode the winds like hawks hunting and ran with the wild coyote. They scurried under brush and slithered like snakes and lizards in the rocks.

The canyon exploded in light and a symphony of creation, destruction and rebirth, erupted all around them. The philosopher said: She's coming alive.

"The canyon is where the crow becomes the hawk, the hawk becomes the eagle, the eagle becomes the thunderbird, and all god's creatures learn to dream," said Jake.

"I understand," said Ruby.

"We are all related," said Jake.

"I understand."

They sat in silence until the sun bathed them in its warmth. Jake folded her in his arms and they rose to breathe it in, the magnitude and the beauty forming an imprint on their minds that would last beyond their breathing lives.

Jake had seen the canyon many times and every time he considered flight as he did now. Ruby grasped his hand in readiness. She knew. She understood.

"Let's go," said Jake finally.

It was not time to fly. It was time to drive. It was not time to bid this world goodbye; it was time to greet the new day and the next adventure.

Ruby sighed, not knowing if she was disappointed or relieved.

A crow emerged from the canyon and cawed. Ruby looked into its eyes and cawed back. The canyon crow entered her soul and promised she would never be alone.

EXTERIOR GRAND CANYON – ARIEL VIEW – SUNRISE

Fade in GLASS ONION.

I told you about the fool on the hill

I tell you man he living there still
Well here's another place you can be
Listen to me.
Fixing a hole in the ocean
Trying to make a dovetail joint – yeah
Looking through a glass onion.

Fade GRAND CANYON. Fade GLASS ONION.

EXTERIOR TWO-LANE HIGHWAY – ARIEL VIEW – MORNING

Ruby and Jake drive.

Fade in A LONG AND WINDING ROAD (The Beatles).

The long and winding road
That leads to your door
Will never disappear
I've seen that road before
It always leads me here
Lead me to your door

Fade WINDING ROAD.

SCENE 11: LAY OF THE LAND

FADE IN:

EXTERIOR LONELY HIGHWAY – DAY

Jake is driving south on a two-lane road, top down, Ruby in the passenger seat.

The Beatles' PIGGIES plays in the foreground.

> *Have you seen the little piggies?*
> *Crawling in the dirt*
> *And for all the little piggies*
> *Life is getting worse*

CLOSE UP of a man in a grey suit, slicked back hair, looking through binoculars. This is one of Guido Lazerri's boys.

> *Have you seen the bigger piggies?*
> *In their starched white shirts*
> *You will find the bigger piggies*
> *Stirring up the dirt*

PAN OUT to Lazerri's boys, two in suits, three in work shirts and khaki slacks, standing around a Monte Carlo and a Buick LaSabre. All are heavily armed.

CLOSE UP of Jake gliding to a stop in the middle of the
road. Jake and Ruby look at each other.

....

Since Sadie Mae was now ruby red instead of baby
blue, Ruby felt she was in need of a new name. She
came up with one when she flipped on the radio and
heard an old rocker song she always loved. Since then,
Sadie Mae was re-christened Cinnamon Girl.

Ruby tossed Jake the keys as they neared the car. It
was a first. Tony always insisted on driving Sadie Mae
as a power trip but she never volunteered. Not once.
Her car was an extension of her soul. It was a private
place where no one else was welcome and those who
entered without an invitation were unwanted
strangers, trespassers, thieves and occupiers. They
deserved whatever cruel fate fell on them.

Jake was different. Everything was different now
and Ruby saw what the situation demanded. She had
the eyes of the crow.

Jake didn't ask why. He took the keys and drove
away from the canyon with an unspoken promise to
return when he had more time to listen and absorb. He
never gave a promise he did not intend to keep. The
canyon was *his* soul and he had never shared it with
anyone before Ruby. He had never felt that anyone
deserved or needed it more than she did.

One way in and one way out, they crossed the
threshold and did not look back. They focused on the
road ahead, knowing there was no place to hide – not

for them or for those who wanted to corner them.

Jake slowed to a stop in the middle of the road. He saw Guido's boys like ants on the wall and he knew they were looking back, waiting for the next move. Leaning forward, Ruby saw them, too. Jake looked at Ruby. Ruby looked at Jake.

"Let's go," she said.

Jake eased forward and leaned on the gas, full speed ahead. Guido's boys scrambled, maneuvering their vehicles to block the road, taking positions behind the blockade and aiming their guns at the maniac speeding toward them.

A few hundred yards in front of the blockade, Jake hit the breaks, sending Cinnamon into a tailspin, her rear tires clipping the dirt and gravel on the side of the road, raising a cloud of dust that washed over Guido's boys like rolling thunder.

"Watch out, mother fuckers!" yelled Ruby, standing in the car. "This is Jake Jones and Ruby Daulton! We don't slow down for nobody! We're mad, we're bad and we're on a mission, baby! So get out of the way or get ready to go down! 'Cause my baby is one mean, lean warrior dog and I'm his sweet honey pie!"

The bullets began to fly as she let out a scream like a tribe of Apache women in a war party. Jake pulled her back to her seat and peeled out the way they came. Two miles down, he took a right on a miner's excursion road, dirt and gravel, heading east.

Guido's boys were in hot pursuit, like a pack of rabid hounds, too pissed to think straight and too stupid to care. Their cars were even more ill suited to a cross-country chase than Ruby's Dodge but there were no more stops. They wanted to kill this skinhead bitch and her monkey boyfriend. They wanted to poke holes in his head and poke Ruby with something else until she begged for death. They no longer cared that Guido and Tony wanted her alive. They wanted to rip her heart out and eat it for lunch.

They knew every syllable Tony and Guido breathed were lies. They knew Tony was a hothead who would not hesitate to blow his own boys away if they made a move on his woman. After what happened in Vegas, they knew Tony set up one of his boys to take the rap so that Guido could deal with Ruby himself. It no longer mattered. Ruby and her man were playing them for fools. It pissed them off. It crossed the line.

Rage transforms smart men into fools and fools into blithering idiots.

Jake glided across the desert just fast enough to keep them in his trail of dust. He pelted them with sand and gravel as Ruby pelted them with words. Mile after mile, their world became a cloud of pounding dirt and sand, their eyes bulging, sweat stinging, hearts pounding, lungs choking, yelling and screaming, shooting at phantoms, too angry to slow down and too stupid to give up the chase.

They were like our soldiers in the sand storm of the Iraq war. Firepower did not matter when your enemy knew the layout. It was the like the Indian wars before the white man decided to kill the buffalo and starve them out. Poison blankets delivered in the form of charity, they cornered the people on reservations and watched them die. Genocide is the only way to win a war against the natives.

There would be no genocide today. Today there would be revenge.

Jake swerved, raising a cloud the size of a bunker buster, turned abruptly to the north, where he spun to a stop on an overhang and watched the two luxury sedans drive over a bluff straight into a gorge, one on top the other.

Ruby got out of the car to observe the carnage. When a couple of the boys emerged, stumbling, spitting and unable to keep their feet, Ruby caught their attention.

"Hey, mother fuckers! I got a message for Tony!"

She raised her fist in a gesture that meant: Up yours!

"I got one for Guido, too! Fuck you!"

She got back in the car, pulled out her purse, and plugged in a CD she picked up back in Phoenix.

"I love you, baby," she said with a kiss.

They drove back to the highway the way they came in, another day and another miracle. Ruby was at the top of her world and Jake was at the top of his game. The CD sang a serenade to their glory and they sang along.

> *I wanna live with a cinnamon girl*
> *I could be happy the rest of my life*
> *With a cinnamon girl*

FADE IN:

EXTERIOR DESERT HIGHWAY – ARIEL VIEW – DAY

Cinnamon kicks up a cloud of dust.

INSERT MONTAGE – WORLD OF CHAOS

NUMBER NINE plays in the foreground.

Guido's boys stumbling around as the cars explode like bombs. Images of dust storms, tornados, hurricanes, bomb attacks, urban war, snipers, suicide bombs, cars burning, charred bodies, crying women and cursing, dark skinned men.

Fade out WORLD OF CHAOS. Fade Number Nine.

Fade in ARIEL VIEW of Jake and Ruby driving.

Fade in CINNAMON GIRL by Neil Young (After the Gold Rush).

Close up of Jake and Ruby singing.

> *A dreamer of pictures I run in the night*
> *You see us together, chasing the moonlight,*
> *My cinnamon girl*

Fade to black.

SCENE 12: DEGANAWIDA'S DRAGONS

FADE IN:

EXTERIOR DESERT HIGHWAY – ARIEL VIEW – DAY

COWGIRL IN THE SAND by Neil Young plays in the foreground as Jake and Ruby drive.

>*Hello cowgirl in the sand*
>*Is this place at your command?*
>*Can I stay here for a while?*
>*Can I see your sweet, sweet smile?*

Jake and Ruby pull up at a Last Chance Gas Station. Ruby makes a call from a pay phone, while Jake fills her up.

NUMBER NINE plays in the background.

Jake and Ruby continue driving east in the desert sun.

>*Hello Ruby in the dust*
>*Has your band begun to rust?*
>*After all the sins we had*
>*I was thinking that we'd turn back*

CLOSE UP of Jake and Ruby singing along.

Old enough now to change your name
When so many love you, is it the same?
It's the woman in you that makes you
Want to play this game

FADE to an elder Indian, cross-legged in the open desert, praying. This is WHITE WOLF, Jake's mentor and spirit guide.

FADE COWGIRL IN THE SAND. FADE IN CORTEZ THE KILLER (Neil Young).

He came dancing across the water
With his galleons and guns
Looking for the new world
In that palace in the sun

....

White Wolf smiled at his favorite student for a long while before they exchanged the embrace of a father and a son. He was not his father. His father was a drunken, gambling, mostly white man, who left him and his mother when he was almost too small to remember. His mother would say he was a good man whose demons were stronger than he was.

His mother passed away before Jake left the reservation. It was one of the reasons he left. She died of a white man's disease born of drinking water poisoned by the nuclear waste buried in Navaho soil. The doctors called it inoperable cancer but he called it the white man's curse. He would have done anything for her. He would have given his life.

He cared for her in her dying days. He prayed at first for her recovery and then for the end of her suffering.   Before she sang her death song she summoned White Wolf and asked him to take care of her son even though she already knew he would. White Wolf filled the space that his father left.

"How long has it been? It seems like yesterday," said the old man.

"It was yesterday," replied Jake, always the coyote.

"I see you brought a gift," said White Wolf, casting a lecherous eye on Ruby, sending a chill straight through her until he gave the joke away with a laugh.

"She has spirit," he said, "for a white woman."

He turned and walked to the shade of a canopy, a sheet of canvas tied to his trailer in a desolate corner of Third Mesa. It seemed to Jake a lonely place until the old man taught him to see without his senses. It was a place of infinite magic if one had the eyes to see.

White Wolf sat at an old wooden table, pouring sage tea as they joined him.

"The old woman is gone to town," he said. "I told her we needed provisions."

Ruby was perplexed. She understood that this was a very old, wise and powerful spirit. She understood the bond between him and Jake.   She did not understand why Jake had not spoken of him. She did not understand that the silence between them spoke more of their bond than words.

The old man was sizing her up and Ruby felt it to the marrow of her bones. When he spoke, she listened as if the balance of all creation hung on his word. Perhaps it did. She was out of her element – a lifetime removed from city lights, jazz clubs, rock and roll, convenience stores and fast food restaurants. Still, there was something comforting in the desert landscape, the solitary mountains and red rock formations, the endless waves of sand and sage rolling with the winds of change. It freed her mind to expand and wander.

She imagined survival in this desolate land, splitting cacti for water, hunting rabbits with stones, eating flowers and finding herbal remedies. She imagined herself the lizard, emerging from shadow to snare a beetle. She imagined herself the hawk, surveying her territory and sounding a warning for human invaders. She imagined herself the coyote, hunting rabbits and field mice, gliding without effort over a floor of sand and stone.

"The coyote is the most adaptable of animals," said White Wolf.

She looked at the old man, rambling on about the weather, the oppressive heat, heat that drove scorpions and rattlesnakes to seek refuge indoors, plants that blocked their path, and she understood that the spoken word was not the message. She looked at Jake, nodding and sipping tea, and she understood the layers of communication that did not depend on spoken words.

She felt the desert pulling at her soul, sucking the essence of her being into its embrace and becoming a part of her as she became a part of the desert. She saw in their faces that the old man and the young mestizo (that was the word they used to describe his mixed bloodline), her dark skinned lover and guardian spirit, understood the transformation that was taking hold of her and approved.

Ruby was becoming someone else. No, she was discovering another spirit within herself. She was learning to see the world with new eyes, silent eyes, eyes of the heart and soul. She was learning not to question what she did not understand. She was learning to trust the goodness of spirit, the warmth of kindness, and mindset of acceptance.

"There is only today," she told herself. Tomorrow does not exist. There is only now: Jake Jones, Ruby Daulton and their teacher, White Wolf of Third Mesa.

"There are no white wolves in the desert," she thought.

The white wolf is a native of the northern woods, where the cold winds blow pure and clean. Like the white buffalo, it is a rare being, rare even in the north. In the desert, it does not exist.

"White Wolf does not belong," she thought.

When he was a child, White Wolf combined a gentle touch with a firm hand. He was strong in mind and body, certain of his way, yet always sensitive to the needs of those weaker and less certain. He was always willing to help the outcast, the unfortunate, the sick and needy. He was not of the world to which he was born. For these reasons, he was given the name of White Wolf and it was prophesied he would become a great teacher to the children of the desert.

Tall Woman, his wife who was short in stature, returned to give Jake and Ruby a warm welcome before she withdrew to prepare a meal worthy of their guests.

When night fell and they were fed and seated comfortably by the fire, the old man told the story of Deganawida's Three Dragons. Deganawida was the great Iroquois prophet and founder of the Six Nations of the northeast.

"He was a man of infinite wisdom," White Wolf proclaimed. "He spoke of the three dragons only days before he left his people for the other world. He spoke at this time so the people would never forget, so they would pass his words to the next generation and so on, so they would feel his words in their souls."

Jake poured fresh tea as White Wolf closed his eyes, inviting the spirits to refresh his vision, though he had told the story a thousand times before.

"One day there appeared a great white dragon. Deganawida did not say where this dragon came from. It did not come from the north for that is where the red dragon came to do battle with the white dragon. It did not come from the south for that is where the black dragon appeared and changed into a white woman, who empowered an Iroquois boy to defeat both the red and white dragons. It did not come from the east for that is where Deganawida himself appeared in the form of a blinding light that frightened all the dragons into submission. So we surmise that the white dragon came from the west, where the Cherokee say all souls go to die."

The four of them sipped their tea and gazed into the fire where the flames danced to the tale of the dragons. The desert wind rose up and swept around them as the barren earth came alive in a spirit of awakening. To each of them it sang a different song, told a different story and delivered a different message.

"What does it mean?" said Ruby at length.

Tall Woman exploded in gales of laughter, nearly spilling her tea as the others joined in her good humor.

"The white dragon should have come from the north," said the old woman.

"The white man should have come from the east but that is where Deganawida appears," said the old man.

"The red dragon should have come from the south. It is the color of fire, the heart and the blood pumping through our veins," said Jake. "It belongs to the south, the birthing place where all life emerges."

"The black dragon," said Tall Woman, "changes into a white woman. She should have been an Indian. The light of a new beginning should have come from the west, not the east."

"Nothing in Deganawida's story makes sense," said White Wolf. "I believe he was teaching his people to see the world with new eyes."

"How does the story end?" pressed Ruby.

"The native people survive by taking in the good parts of the dragons that threatened them with destruction," said White Wolf.

Ruby wanted to ask what happened to the dragons but she found her mind drifting away. Jake guided her to a bed of buffalo hide and furs in the corner of the room where they laid in each other's arms and set their minds free to wander.

It was time to let go the waking world. It was time to dream.

Many times I've been alone and many times I've cried
Any way you'll never know the many ways I've tried

But still they lead me back to the long winding road
You left me standing here a long, long time ago
Don't leave waiting here
Lead me to your door

SCENE 13: LIZARD DREAMS

FADE IN:

EXTERIOR DESERT HIGHWAY – ARIEL VIEW – DAY

CRYSTAL SHIP by Jim Morrison plays in the foreground as Jake and Ruby awaken in the desert trailer of White Wolf and Tall Woman. REVOLUTION 9 plays in the background.

> *The days are bright and filled with pain*
> *Enclose me in your gentle rain*
> *The time you ran was too insane*

INSERT MONTAGE – DISTORTED DREAM VISIONS

CLOSE UP of the eyes of the crow, yielding to a series of distorted visions: A rabbit captured in the claws of a hawk, coyote on the prowl, a wolf emerging from fire, full moon in a darkened sky, a dead soldier on desert sand, fire in the sky, a wall of water washing over the land.

> *Oh tell me where your freedom lies*
> *The streets are fields that never die*

Deliver me from reasons why

Number nine, number nine, number nine…

Fade Dream Vision.

....

From a basin of honeysuckle water, they washed their hands and faces, sending a shockwave through their senses. The smell of sage permeated the air while White Wolf and Tall Woman, a smile of the heart imprinted on their faces and a childlike twinkle in their eyes, handed them mugs of fresh coffee to warm their hands and blankets to dull the chill until the heat of the fire took hold.

White Wolf drew the deerskin curtains on the eastern window to allow the first light of day to break through like a beacon to their souls.

They sat in silence, feeling no need to offer commentary on a shared experience. Ruby alone fought back the instinct to fill the silence with words, to test the validity of her perceptions by the testimony and confirmation of her fellow travelers. Old habits die kicking and screaming like a pony must learn to accept a rider. Dry lands swallow the rain and old leaders fight back the inevitable waves of change. It is the way of nature and the manner of humankind.

Soon the cool of morning gave way to a dry desert heat as they fed on a mixture of ground corn and oatmeal, sweetened with honey and blended with water into a paste. They finished their coffee, folded their blankets, and followed the old man out the door and deep into the barren desert.

White Wolf stopped, as if the spirits commanded him, looked to the sky, reached into a leather pouch at his hip, and held it aloft. He howled as a werewolf would do in the full of the moon, yapped as a coyote prancing, and danced in a small circle, chanting without words until he circled four times. He released the herbal medicine in the four directions, then above, then below and then to the heart. It was a completion of the sacred circle in the seven sacred directions.

He turned to Jake, offering the medicine of the pouch.

"I have sung my starting song," he said. "Now you must sing."

Jake took the leather pouch, held it to his lips and pressed it to his heart. He opened the pouch and extracted a pinch. As the old man had done, he howled, yapped and cawed until he came to the dance. Where the old one's dance was heavy and pounding like the wolf, Jake's was light and fleeting like a bird, then swift like a lizard. Where White Wolf's song had wailed and moaned, Jake's was sharp and crisp. When he finished, he released the medicine in the seven directions and stood beside his mentor.

Ruby stood petrified in awe and wondered if she was the butt of an Indian joke. She was a white chick, a Vegas party girl, and though she wanted to believe in the honor that was being offered, it all seemed too unreal.

They seemed to share her amusement with knowing smiles but continued staring in silence, the old man holding out his offering.

"Alright," she said. "Believe me, I've done a million

things stranger."

She stepped forward, took the medicine bag and performed the ritual as Jake had done. When she reached the dance stage, she felt a spirit enfold her. She was a dancer but this was different. It was the dance of the coyote and the flight of the crow, playful, joyous and filled with yearning. She yapped and cawed and completed the ritual with an offering in the seven directions and took her place next to White Wolf, who nodded his approval.

They followed him into the ocean of sand, waves slowly rolling beneath their feet, wind whispering harmonies, hearts beating as drums, an oppressive blanket of heat washing over them, sparing them, leaving them to complete their journey.

With the sun still high in the sky, they constructed a shelter from found wood and brush, laid a circle of stones, and made camp. They would light a fire at sunset. Until then, they would sit and wait. They passed the time drinking tea and exploring their surroundings one by one. They were perched on a cliff overlooking a vast expanse of the Navaho desert, etched with gullies, crevices and towering rock monuments, the markings of an earth in constant motion.

Everything from the billowy white clouds above to the lonely coyote scurrying on the desert floor below, from the face of an ancestor carved in stone to the caw of an unseen crow, seemed somehow familiar and inviting – as if it had always been here waiting for this moment.

As the sun crashed on the western horizon, White Wolf sat before the circle of stones and began to chant in the tongue of the ancients. Jake and Ruby joined him, finding a language they could not have learned, a language that was stored in the sand and stones, unleashed by the power of prayer.

Each in turn rose to follow a path that belonged only to one. Jake moved to the south, toward a cluster of rock formations, eyes open but his vision blurred, dream walking. The spirits guided him to his place of power, an indentation atop a round boulder, and there he sat, entering the shadow land where light and darkness meet, blending the worldly with the ethereal stars. He became the lizard and the desert became the kingdom of his dream.

Ruby resisted the call until a sensation of warmth entered her spirit. She rose and felt herself pulled to the edge of the cliff. She fought back but the sensation of comfort flowed over and within her until she yielded and followed down a thin finger of stone extending outward over the great expanse. She was the crow flying above her desert domain. Down below she saw a coyote gliding gracefully across the land. She was the coyote, stopping to gaze at the crow above.

She was gripped by a fear of being watched, pursued, hunted, and found herself transported to the streets of a city, where the sounds of jazz and celebration permeated the moving throng of smiling, yelling, staggering people. She looked up to see a face staring down at her from behind a mask.

It was the French Quarters in New Orleans.

She turned south to see a sky filled with rage. She closed her eyes and heard the earth rumble like a thousand pounding trains. She saw earthen levees tear and break, streets filled with angry waves of water, people swept away, trapped in attics and stranded on rooftops. They cried out for help but no one heard their call. They gathered together and suffered the indignity of a forgotten tribe. Ruby suffered with them and fought back her tears. She understood their need for the strength of warriors, not the comfort of priests.

The old man called them back to the fire with the cry of a wolf. They embraced him in silence and sat gazing into the dancing flames, lost in the wonder of another world.

"Great Spirit," he said, "we thank you for the guidance and the wisdom and the powers we have received this night. We thank you for the gift of sight.

"I am the wolf, the teacher, and the sleeping bear. This night I have howled at the moon and received its mystery. I have known the beauty of being alone with my thoughts. I have learned the oneness of all beings, none lesser nor greater than myself. For this and all the things I cannot give words, I thank you."

He gave an offering of earth in the seven directions and bowed his head.

"I am the lizard," said Jake, "the dreamer and the dragonfly of illusions. Tonight I have lived in the shadows and witnessed wonders beyond words. I have seen through layers of illusion to the heart of all beings. For this vision I give thanks."

He gave his offering and bowed his head.

Ruby focused on the flames, her soul open and unafraid, her mind clear, until the spirit moved her to speak.

"I am the crow and the coyote. Tonight I have run in the shadows of moonlight, hunted and tasted flesh. I have known the fear of being hunted. I have seen the circle of life and followed the path of destiny. For this I am grateful beyond words."

She gave an offering, as Jake and White Wolf had, and bowed her head in silent meditation. When she raised it again, everything around her had changed. A strange, visible glow enveloped everything in sight. The rocks, the sand and brush, everything moved and breathed in the rhythm of life.

Though sentient memories would fade in time, nothing would ever be the same. Ruby revered it and held to it as if her future, her soul, her place in the world depended on remembering every detail and breathing it in.

Jake and White Wolf were deep in meditation, sensing the same need for complete understanding and appreciation.

Ruby remembered New Orleans and wondered, with a sharp tinge of sorrow that cut straight to the heart, how long it would be before destiny summoned.

When they returned to the trailer in the early morning, four armed warriors greeted them. White men with greasy hair had come to the reservation and were offering money for Ruby and Jake. The warriors were here to warn them and protect them. They would camp here until the danger passed.

White Wolf welcomed them with open arms. They ate and talked about hard times on the reservation: no jobs, no recreation for the children, homes without heat or air conditioning, schools with books from the sixties that spoke of the genocide as manifest destiny, disease, drugs and alcohol. It was a time of war and many of their young were signing up to fight in Iraq.

"They say it's in our blood," said a woman with mourning eyes. "They say we can prove ourselves through battle. I say they send us to fight against our own people, indigenous people. I say there is no honor in the white man's wars."

"They come back changed," said a man who might have been Jake's brother. "They come back cold and hard and turn to the bottle."

"Or they don't come back at all," said another.

Someone mentioned a story she had read in the paper describing a killing field south of the border around Nogales. Dozens if not hundreds of women were killed and buried in shallow graves. Ruby knew then why Jake would not cross the southern border. She understood that he had saved her life once more.

When night fell, Ruby told Jake it was time for her to go but she understood if he wanted to stay. This was his home and these were his people. She wanted him to go with her but she would not stand in the way of his happiness. Jake replied that he would go with her as long as the Great Spirit gave its blessing. Ruby embraced him in loving arms and held him close.

In the morning, White Wolf led them outside to where Cinnamon was parked next to an old well-worn Ford pickup.

"I like this vehicle," he said, placing his hand on Ruby's Dodge. "I was wondering if you'd like to trade her."

It was a done deal though it pulled at Ruby's heart. She loved that car. They had traveled many miles together but they needed a new vehicle to get past Guido's thugs. They needed function, not form. They needed to blend with the land.

"Does the radio work?" she asked.

"Like a million bucks," said White Wolf.

"Deal," said Ruby.

They shook hands and embraced with the warmth of relatives.

"Take care of my son," White Wolf whispered. "There is a place in his heart only you can heal."

It would be a long time before she understood his words. She would think of them every day of their adventure and ponder the meaning. They made their goodbyes, started up the old truck and headed east into a new day.

FADE IN:

EXTERIOR DESERT BACKROAD – ARIEL VIEW – DAY

An old gray pickup leaves a trail of dust.

CLOSE UP of Ruby in the passenger seat, a tear rolling down her cheek.

Neil Young's IT'S A DREAM (Prairie Wind) plays in the foreground.

> *It's a dream, it's only a dream*
> *And it's fading now, fading away*

> *It's a dream, it's only a dream*
> *Just a memory without anywhere to stay*

Fade out IT'S A DREAM. Fade in LUCY IN THE SKY

WITH DIAMONDS as they drive on down the road.

INSERT MONTAGE: THE NEON DESERT

A liquid desert in bright neon with close-ups of the lizard, the crow and coyote.

> *Picture yourself in a boat on a river*
> *With tangerine trees and marmalade skies*
> *Somebody calls you, you answer quite slowly*
> *A girl with kaleidoscope eyes*
>
> *Cellophane flowers of yellow and green*
> *Towering over your head*
> *Look for the girl with the sun in her eyes*
> *And she's gone*
>
> *Lucy in the sky with diamonds...*

Fade out.

SCENE 14: THE LAND OF OZ

FADE IN:

EXTERIOR HIGHWAY – DRIVER'S VIEW – DAY

IT'S A DREAM (from Neil Young's *Prairie Wind*) slowly fades as THE PAINTER (same album) slowly comes to the foreground. The land is changing from the sandy desert of Third Mesa to the windblown plains and farmlands of Oklahoma and Kansas.

> *Green to green, red to red*
> *Yellow to yellow in the light*
> *Black to black when the evening comes*
> *Blue to blue in the night*

INTERIOR PICKUP – RUBY'S VIEW – NEARING SUNSET

Close up of JAKE, eyes on the road, driving, as Ruby studies him.

> *It's a long road behind me*
> *It's a long road ahead*
> *If you follow every dream*
> *You might get lost*

Fade out THE PAINTER. Fade in REVOLUTION 9.

Number nine, number nine, number nine…

....

They were rolling down Highway 160, as fast as the old truck could take them without shaking their bones loose, the desert flatlands giving way to soft hills and dales, the browns and reds of the earth to the greens and yellows of grass, trees, fields of wheat, corn and alfalfa, from the random richness of nature to the ordered markings of man.

The route would take them through Ulysses (the civil war hero and president who authorized the genocidal wars on the Lakota and Nez Perce) and Hickok (the legendary lawman and gambler who served as a scout to Custer's Seventh Calvary), where they would head north through the Buffalo Game Reserve to Garden City, Kansas, home of Ruby's grandmother and the land of her childhood dreams.

Ruby had no childhood – not really. Her father left when she was a girl and only years later did she remember how abusive he had been. To this day there were chapters she would not fill. All but erased from her memories, events would emerge as scattered images like a reflection in a broken mirror and dive back into deep shadows before the meaning could be grasped. Her mother was always obsessed with the wrong kinds of men, drugs and alcohol. Ruby survived to her teenage years when she broke out of her shell, the self imposed prison of her emotions, to claim her space in the world. She was pronounced incorrigible and shipped off to her grandparents in Garden City. By the time she finished high school and set out on her own, she had lost contact with her mother, her father, her stepfather and everyone else with a family connection – even her grandparents whom she loved more than life.

Since her grandfather died several years back, her grandmother was the only family Ruby had and now, with the prospect of death in her mind and its shadow on her trail, she felt a burning desire, after leaving Third Mesa, to take her in her arms, to hold her once more, to look into the mirror of time and to rekindle the dying flame of family.

"I've been meaning to ask you something," said Ruby.

"What's that?"

"When I picked you up back in California, I could have sworn you were broke."

Jake laughed. "I won a bet in Vegas."

"That was you, the royal flush?"

Jake nodded. "In hearts."

"Why aren't we on a plane to Aruba?"

"I only had a dollar," he explained.

"Figures," Ruby reflected. She studied him as if he was a player, to see if she could read him. "You like to gamble, Jake?"

"Like the white man says," he smiled, "all Indians love to gamble...only I hate to lose."

Ruby's mind raced ahead like a flash of lightning on the horizon. There was a riverboat casino that ran from St. Louis to New Orleans. She had seen pictures and dreamed of a cruise down the Mississippi with all the comforts, flash and excitement of Las Vegas. If they played their cards right, they could build a stake to lay down a claim in the Big Easy.

"You've got to believe, baby," she said. "Believing is everything. I've seen a man knock down a bull, a crow fly like an eagle, and a little girl stare down a beast the size of a bear. The power of believing is everything."

Jake knew at a glance Ruby was on a roll and there was no stopping her. She had a plan and she would stick to it like moths to a lonely light bulb.

"We head over to St. Louis, catch the Mississippi Queen and head on down to New Orleans. We hit 'em on the Queen, hit 'em in New Orleans, head on over to Biloxi and him 'em again. The sky's the limit, baby, and we're rolling nothing but sevens!"

"Whatever you say, baby."

"No, Jake, I'm serious. You have to believe."

He gave her time to examine him like a mystified doctor until she grasped the depth of his sincerity. There was no need for persuasion. He was with her as long as the spirits approved. Even then, if it should ever arise, he would never leave her until she was safe. It was a delicate balance: assuring her safety and honoring her instincts.

"I believe in you, Ruby. I believe."

Jake and Ruby: nothing could stop them. They had the magic of destiny and the medicine of the crow. They were a force of nature, undeniable and pure. Like Bonnie and Clyde, Cisco and Poncho, Butch Cassidy and the Sundance Kid, they were bound for glory on the road of adventure and nothing but nothing could stand in their way.

"Got a wide open road and a wide open sky! Got the four winds blowing through the cracks in my mind! Got the sun shining bright and my eyes wide open! Mercury's in the house of wonder and my baby's got a crow on his shoulder! What more can a woman ask?"

She edged over to Jake, put her arms around his shoulders, pressed her body against him and tickled his ear with her breath.

"What do you say we pull in to the next motel? Grandma can wait," she whispered.

Rounding a slow curve, Jake happily obliged, checking into cabin number nine at the inevitable Sleepy Time motel. Life was good. The muses were dancing, the graces were singing and the gods were in their rightful places.

They spent the sweet hours of night making love and the rest of the time playing poker over chips and beer. Ruby taught him all she knew: Tell signs, markers, who to play against and who to play with, when to play slow and when to go for the kill. She came to the conclusion he had natural talent. Some folks are born with the gift and Jake was one of them. He was hard to read, easy to misread and impossible to play for a fool.

"Have you ever been in love?" she asked as he settled in the grip of her embrace.

"I'm in love with you," he replied.

"Have you ever been in love before?" she asked.

He had known love before but it burned in his heart. It was a love that took root in his gut and haunted his soul. It was more than a year since her passing but not a day passed without a glance, a smile, a word, the sight of a yellow moon, or the turning of a page reminded him of her. In so many ways, Ruby reminded him of her. Love reminded him. Passion reminded him. The softness of her touch and the pull of her loins reminded him of her. Everything reminded him until he prayed to let go, to let her memory be washed away, to let her love be buried in the sea of yesterday.

"I'm in love with Ruby Daulton here and now," he said and he said no more.

Ruby let it go. She knew what it was like to have painful memories summoned against her will. She was familiar with the need to bury the past. Friends had often said she should confront her ghosts, her demons, and her dark memories. She should let them out in the open and slay them like dragons. But what if the dragons consumed her? Maybe some day she would take their advice but not today. For now she would keep them hidden away and channel the pain into something useful – singing and dancing and living life without regrets. If it was good enough for her it was good enough for Jake. Maybe it was the key to the bond that held them together.

They slept a few hours, awoke with clear minds, and covered the last stretch of asphalt to grandma's house and the Land of Oz. Ruby was glowing. The radiance of her spirit made the bright Kansas sun pale and tepid by comparison. Destiny's child, Alice in Wonderland, Dorothy and her ruby red slippers, the magic and wonder and beauty of believing.

On the road to Garden City, at the turnoff to grandma's house, four crows greeted them on a telephone line, scattering in all directions as they passed. Jake looked at Ruby but saw that she was already gone, on a journey of memories. In her life in LA or Las Vegas, she never mentioned her family. She told her friends she was an orphan, transferred from foster home to foster home from Chicago to Seattle. She never spoke of her childhood and no one ever pressed her.

The bond between Ruby and her grandmother was profound yet foreboding. Ruby had a keen sense of fear. What was she afraid of? Afraid of losing her last connection to the bloodline? Afraid of not belonging? Afraid of losing the innocence of unconditional love? Afraid of being captured by love and losing her independence, her inimitable free spirit?

She remembered dancing over lawn sprinklers on hot summer days, playing with imaginary playmates, opening her eyes to see her grandmother's loving smile through the kitchen window. She remembered rag dolls, the breakfast of champions, Malto o Meal, hot chocolate, cowgirl coffee, fudge brownies and oatmeal cookies. She remember falling asleep, dreaming of boyfriends and wild adventures, safe in her grandmother's arms.

Ruby smiled in reflection and tears suddenly streamed from her eyes. Jake pulled over and held her until the trembling subsided.

"Something has happened," she said.

Jake already knew. He saw the shadow of death surround her like a thick mist in a dark forest. Ruby did not believe in death. She believed it was only a passage, a doorway, a simple transformation of the life spirit, a turning of the great wheel or the endless cycle of eternal existence. She believed that good people would be blessed in transformation and bad people would be cursed. She knew that her grandmother would be blessed but she yearned to see her one last time, if only to say thank you and goodbye, if only to tell her she loved her with every piece of her shattered heart.

When they pulled up to the old farmhouse, there were cars parked in the gravel driveway, children playing quietly in the shade of a willow, faces long with grief and through the window Ruby's long lost mother, painted in sorrow.

They walked into the shadow of mourning and Ruby's mother gasped, taking hold of Ruby's hands, whispering, "She's been asking for you."

She walked to the bedroom door as the world turned gray and slowed to a crawl, as if prayers could hold back time and the hand of god. She swallowed the bitter pill of fate and bit down hard on her lower lip as if pain could ease her sorrow.

She saw death in her grandmother's eyes. In that moment, she was gone and Ruby saw the light. A fluttering butterfly, a soaring bird of prey, rounding its way to heaven's gate, and the smiling, radiant face of love.

"Maemah," she whispered. "I love you."

"Sweet child," her grandmother said. "I love you with all my heart."

Her hand reached out to grasp Ruby's and then she was gone. Her mission complete, her last act of love a final goodbye to her favorite child.

It was beyond Ruby's control and beyond her comprehension. She made peace with her mother, listened to stories of affection, and heard someone say, "There's no place like home." She had found her way to the Land of Oz and the eternal dream of belonging but she did not belong here and she knew she never would.

"Where's Jake?" she asked suddenly.

"He went for a walk about an hour ago," someone said.

Ruby found him sitting in the bed of the pickup, back to the cab.

"What are you up to, Sailor?"

Jake was in a daze, swimming in a sea of chaos, particles of random energy, molecular disarray, spirals of starlight, concentric circles of self-consuming thought, mind over body, body over mind, the fire of all existence like a magnet to his soul.

"I was watching the stars," he replied, "and it occurred to me: Maybe Einstein didn't discover relativity. Maybe he invented it."

Ruby laughed until she cried and wiped away the tears. The workings of his mind were the greatest of all mysteries.

"Thanks for that, Jake."

"You have a choice," he said. "You have a home and family."

Ruby looked at the house of her grandparents, a house that was once filled with love and kindness, and caught the glancing eye of her mother.

"You're right about that, Jake," she replied, "but it isn't here."

She took the wheel as Jake jumped in the passenger's side, and they drove off into a warm, silent Kansas night. Fate took its turn and the adventure continued.

Ruby turned the radio on and hit the dash with her

fist.

FADE IN:

EXTERIOR HIGHWAY – DRIVER'S VIEW – NIGHT

THE LONG AND WINDING ROAD comes to the fore as headlights shine on the dotted line.

> *Many times I've been alone*
> *And many times I've cried*
> *Any way you'll never know*
> *The many times I've tried*
>
> *But still they lead me back*
> *To the long winding road*
> *You left me standing here*
> *A long long time ago*
> *Don't leave me waiting here*
> *Lead me to your door*

Fade WINDING ROAD. Fade highway to black.

We hear softly:

> *Number nine, number nine, number nine…*

Fade out.

SCENE 15: KANSAS CITY BLUES

FADE IN:

EXTERIOR HIGHWAY – STARLIT SKY VIEW –
NIGHT

The stars float by overhead as Jake and Ruby drive the lonesome highway from Oklahoma to Kansas City on their way to St. Louis and a date with the Mississippi Queen. Ruby is heard singing.

> *Going to Kansas City, Kansas City here I come*
> *I'm going to Kansas City, Kansas City here I come*
> *They got a crazy way of lovin' and I wanna get me some*

INTERIOR PICKUP – JAKE – NIGHT

Close up of JAKE, eyes on Ruby singing, dumbfounded and amazed. Close up of RUBY, singing like the reincarnation of Billie Holliday.

> *I was standing on the corner, 12th street and Vine*
> *I was standing on the corner, 12th street and Vine*
> *I got a Kansas City man and a bottle of Kansas City wine*

INTERIOR LIVING ROOM – MORNING

A disheveled man with long hair, a grubby beard and beady eyes in a tattered tee shirt and jeans sits rolling a joint. This is SANTINI. His eyes dart around the room. A revolver is on the coffee table.

Fade out KANSAS CITY. Fade in COME TOGETHER by Lennon and McCartney.

Here come old flattop, he come grooving up slowly
He got joo-joo eyeball, he one holy roller
He got hair down to his knee
Got to be a joker he just do what he please

Fade COME TOGETHER. Fade scene.

....

A taste of the white orchid, the eternal Lady Day, a voice that sprang from the depths of eternal sorrow, but it was not the radio, not a remastered CD; it was the inestimable and unearthly Ruby Daulton. She had a style, a phrasing and tone distinctly her own but it sprang from that same well as the eternal torch singers of a former age and it left Jake devoid of words.

Ruby was a singer's singer. She had the talent, the looks and the flare to fill women with envy and make men fall to their knees. How she ended up running drugs and dancing in two-bit stripper bars was a mystery as deep as the seventh sea, as illusive as a psychedelic dream.

She let the last note drift to the heavens and gave

him a wink and a smile. To her it was as natural as breathing the air, as effortless as walking.

Jake spoke from the depth of his native soul: "You should go straight to New Orleans, Ruby. They'll make you a legend and worship your beauty. You'll never have to hustle another day in your life."

Ruby laughed and leaned out the window to breathe the night air and take in the stars. He wasn't the first to tell her how talented she was and how easy it would be for her in New York, Chicago or New Orleans. But it wasn't easy. It was never easy. Nothing ever came to Ruby without blood and sweat.

"Don't you know what they do to legends in New Orleans?"

Visions of Billie Holliday, eyes rolled back, a needle dangling from her arm, and Bessie Smith dying in the front seat of car, parked outside a white only hospital washed over him. What do you do when the jackhammer of truth slams down on your head?

"Yeah," he reflected. It was a story as old as the mountains and a truth as thick as blood. The good die young and the fates mark the great for tragedy. He knew what they did to legends but what choice did they have?

They had a new plan: a quick stop in Kansas City and on to St. Louis. Catch a ride on the Mississippi Queen, a floating paddleboat casino, straight down to New Orleans and a new life. They would test the fates the old fashioned way: a game of chance. Jake liked the idea. Fresh off a Royal Flush in Hearts, it appealed to his sense of poetry and adventure. The only part that gave him a second thought was the stop in Kansas City.

"In and out," Ruby said of the Kansas City detour. She had some friends there and she felt a need for self-defense. She would score a concealable weapon and find out the latest news from Guido and the boys back in Vegas.

Jake did not object to Ruby having a gun but he was less certain that she should trust anyone connected with her past. If she wanted a gun, she should have got one from White Wolf. Barring that he'd feel better scoring one in a dark alley than tapping her connections in Vegas or LA. It was a chance he wouldn't have taken. He didn't like the odds.

It was early morning when they crossed the state line, stumbled into Kansas City and navigated their way across town to Truman Avenue at 38th Street. The numbers were coming up wrong and Ruby was reading the signs. Jake was back in his sleeping mode; even when he was awake, he was asleep. She had a long conversation with his subconscious, in which he spoke in tongues, riddles and rhymes, eyes rolling and head swaying from side to side.

"Tell me about your mother," Ruby said.

"The earth was shaken to her core," replied the sleeping man. "The clouds were dark, shivering rain. The ocean is plasma, a magnetic swarm, flies so thick, the caretaker warned: the milk is poison."

His eyes rolled and sweat covered his brow but when Ruby became concerned, he would break into poetry, rolling out a velvet tribute to the beauty of life.

Ruby was both amused and amazed at the workings of Jake's sleeping mind but now that they were nearing her Kansas City connection, she sensed danger and felt the need for his conscious presence.

She drove half a block past the apartment building and parked. They were friends of a friend, every bit as dubious as Jake feared, but it seemed reasonable until now. The same instincts that told her she needed a gun now warned her to be wary. She needed Jake to take the ball, bounce it around, and figure out which way to move.

She shook him hard and pleaded with him to wake up. His eyes rolled behind closed lids before springing wide open, as if petrified: "Nanih waiyah!" he called out and then lapsed back into his world of dreams.

She pressed her body against him and teased him with a kiss. Again, his eyes rolled and popped open in fear. It was strange. She had never seen fear in him while he was awake but here it was in his dreams.

A stranger in a strange land, Jake heard Ruby's voice and crawled out of the abyss, fluttering his eyes, adjusting to an unfamiliar world, until he saw her shining face.

"What is nonny wayuh?" she asked.

"Nanih waiyah," he muttered. "It's Choctaw for the fox."

"The fox and the weasel," said Ruby. It was what Sister Woman called the couple in Kansas City, the connection she was about to meet.

The fox was a master of camouflage, a wearer of masks, renowned for cunning, while the weasel was known for stealth and an ability to see beyond disguise. They were a perfect match for all the wrong reasons. Ruby was having doubts.

"What were you afraid of?" Ruby asked.

"What is anyone afraid of?" Jake replied. "The unknown, the unfamiliar, the tunnel of darkness, the absence of light."

"I've never seen you afraid before."

"You've never brought me back from so far under."

Ruby's mind raced in a thousand directions at once but everything would have to wait. She had to focus on the moment and she needed Jake to be there with her, here and now.

"We need a plan," she said.

"We have a plan," replied Jake. "We go in, keep our eyes open, you make the deal and we get out."

"It's not much of a plan," said Ruby.

"I've got another plan," said Jake. "We head on to St. Louis and take our chances."

"No," Ruby reflected. "We don't back down. Once you start, you never stop."

It was becoming an obsession but Jake wouldn't fight it now. It was what made her Ruby Daulton. It was one reason he would go to the wall for her.

"Watch my back side," she said as she stepped from the truck.

Jake followed, emptying his mind and proceeding in the quiet manner of the fox, ready for another appointment with destiny. Ruby hesitated like a cornered cat, her palms sweating, her movements stuttered and quick.

"Relax," said Jake as she pressed the buzzer on the floor level.

A man with long dark hair and beady eyes circled in darkness greeted them at the door. Jake smiled. He looked like a weasel. His weak chin shadowed by a thin beard gave the impression that his face converged at the end of his prominent, pointy nose. He wore tattered blue jeans and a ragged Aerosmith tee shirt, wiping his eyes and scratching himself as his eyes darted back and forth.

"Santini?" Ruby inquired.

"Yeah," he replied, motioning them in, closing and bolting the door behind them.

"Who's this?" he muttered.

"A friend," said Ruby.

The weasel squinted as he looked Jake in the eyes, trying to measure the threat.

"Coffee?" he asked on his way to the kitchen, overrun with dishes and discarded packaging from Chinese takeout and pizza delivery.

"Sure," said Ruby.

Jake took it in. The man who drew all eyes at a motorcycle bar in Arizona was suddenly invisible, like the Indian in *One Flew Over the Cuckoo's Nest*. The weasel could not see through him. He figured he was too dumb to talk.

Santini yelled "Cat!" as he poured the coffee and served them in the cluttered space of a small living room. "Get the hell up, your friends are here!"

Cat the fox came in with an open silk gown and a platter of cocaine with four lines drawn and a cut straw. She was a striking woman with short jet-black hair and long, thin lines. Jake deferred but Ruby and the weasel indulged. Cat snorted the extra.

On the face of it, Cat was far too attractive to be attached to the weasel without an angle. She was putting on airs of nicety, which was unnatural for a low stakes transaction in the morning hours. Jake sensed something was on and this was nothing more than a charade.

"I need a gun," Ruby pressed.

"What's your hurry?" purred the fox.

"Business before pleasure," replied Ruby.

"A little late for that," said Cat with a snort.

"Have you got the goods?"

"Sure," said Cat. "Relax. Hey baby, show 'em what you've got."

The weasel cleared his nostrils, displayed a crooked grin and went to the bedroom, closing the door behind him. After a moment too long, Ruby looked at Jake and Jake looked back at Ruby. The gig was up. The weasel emerged with a metal briefcase displaying four handguns, ranging from a snub nose to a pearl-handled derringer.

Ruby grabbed the latter and asked, "How much do I owe you?"

"It's clean," said the weasel. "I'll take three hundred."

"Is it loaded?"

Santini drew another line, pulled a box of bullets from a desk drawer, and tossed them on the table. Ruby loaded the derringer and drew a bead on Cat's forehead.

"What's the news from Vegas, sweetheart?"

"Take it easy, Ruby. No one knows where you are."

"They didn't before I came here."

Ruby tossed three hundred on the table and backed toward the door as the weasel angled for the gun stashed behind his back.

"You pull that thing," said Jake, "you'd better be good."

Jake had his knife in his hand and Santini froze. Weasels are good liars and cheats but they're not good killers. They lack the instinct.

Back in the truck, Ruby took stock. She had a gun but the bad guys knew where they were. If they had any sense at all, they probably had a hunch where they were headed.

"Damn baby, that was mistake."

"We're alive." shrugged Jake. "Let's roll."

Jake was asleep by the time they hit the interstate, dreaming of Mississippi starlight on ink black waters, drowning souls in liquid tombs, forever wanting, yearning, reaching for the light. Liquid nightmares and sparkling fireflies, loves lost and prayers unanswered, betrayals, dark deals, a man with smiling eyes and lightning lies, illusions and deception. A million souls sacrificed to muddy graves beneath a blood red sky, the suffering innocent and desperate cries. There is light in shadow and darkness in light. There is right in wrong and wrong in right. It was a conundrum and a warning, a vision of foreboding.

"Wasichu!" said Jake from the depths of sleep. "The Killing Spirit!" he mumbled. "The Killing Spirit!"

Ruby let him sleep and wept as she drove. It was all wrong. She cursed herself for letting her ego better her common sense. Jake warned her and she threw it off like swatting a fly. A summer rain began to fall and it fell in gales of darkness.

"Damn baby, that was a mistake."

INTERIOR PICKUP – RUBY – DAY

Close up of RUBY crying as the rain comes pouring down. The sky darkens, as if the entire world has fallen under a cloud.

Fade in COME TOGETHER.

> *He bag production, he got walrus gumboot*
> *He got Ono sideboard, he one spinal cracker*
> *He got feet down below his knee*
> *Hold you in his armchair you can feel his disease*

As Jake sleeps, Ruby wipes the tears from her face and sings.

> *Going to Kansas City, Kansas City here I come*
> *I'm going to Kansas City, Kansas City here I come*
> *They got a crazy way of lovin' and I wanna get me some*

Fade to black.

SCENE 16: MISSISSIPPI BLACK

FADE IN:

EXTERIOR – MOONLIT WATERS – NIGHT

We hear the haunting voice of Jim Morrison and The
Doors singing…

> *You're lost, little girl*
> *You're lost, little girl*
> *Tell me who are you, dear?*

Through the dark waters, just below the surface, we see
floating corpses, eyes open and testifying to horror.

INTERIOR – ST. LOUIS BAR – DAY

From above, we see the crack and scatter of billiard
balls as the eight ball settles in focus.

> *We think that you know what to do*
> *You're lost, little girl*

Fade scene.

....

On the passenger side of the old truck, Jake tossed and turned, moaning and groaning, like a man in agony. It was too much to ignore. Ruby pulled over at a highway rest stop and awakened him just outside of St. Louis.

"What is it, baby?"

A dance with the devil in the deep dark sea, something was holding him down, his arms tied behind him as he clawed and crawled toward the light of Ruby's voice. His throat gripped tight and a fear of drowning overwhelmed him.

"Talk to me, baby."

There is an element of the human species that would sacrifice humanity and the sanctity of life for the mere joy of observing the terror as it spreads from one innocent soul to the next in a chain reaction of fear. There is a part of us all that has an endless thirst, a hunger, a dark gripping need that can never be satisfied or satiated. It cowers in shadows and avoids reflections not for fear of what it does not reflect but fear of what it does.

Subsumed by the black waters of the Mississippi he sensed that only Ruby could rescue him. She kissed his rolling eyes and lips, wiped the sweat from his brow and pulled at his loins to awaken him. His eyes flickered open like the fluttering wings of a butterfly and Ruby pulled him in, holding him to her beating heart.

"What's wrong, baby?"

He could only shake his head, clearing his mind and adjusting to light. He still had the clear sensation of drowning but it was Ruby he saw sinking into the void. There was something in those waters that both summoned and threatened her.

"Something dark," he said, knowing Ruby would never turn back.

Destiny was in charge and the Mississippi was destiny's chosen path. The nightmare was a warning meant for him; it told him to be alert and vigilant. There was a darkness hovering over Ruby's life and her soul was in peril.

They drove on with the darkness growing around them until they pulled into a Holliday Inn, booked room 909, and paid cash for the night. They would not rush to meet fate's embrace. They would take their time, embrace the moment and greet whatever waited with open eyes, defiant and steady like a rock.

Ruby opened the curtains and gazed at the city skyline, clustered towers and the St. Louis arch. They ordered room service and drank to the glory of life on earth, making love in moonlight on the motel floor, bathing in each other's desires, sharing sensual dreams and lustful fantasies.

When two bodies destined to ignite, come together in the moonlight, angels dance in heaven and sirens serenade. No words could reach the divine essence, the eternal flame and insoluble mystery of love and lust at a crossroads. Their senses tuned to a collective heartbeat, they drank the warmth and texture of the flesh, taste, tongue and soul.

They feasted until the strength of their bodies succumbed to a driving need for release and rebirth: Sleep pulled at them like a stone in black water.

A stone in black water.

They awoke to the clear blue skies of a bright summer day in the city of the grand arch and turned their backs on the world surrounding them. The Mississippi Queen would dock at sunset but the day belonged to them. They would not think ahead or look behind. They would live in the moment completely.

Together they explored second hand shops, cafes and bookstores in old St. Louis, buying costumes for the Queen. By late afternoon, they settled in a workingman's bar with a couple of pool tables, a line of video poker machines, and a long bar with backless stools.

Jake had the discomforting feeling that someone followed them. He could feel their eyes hiding in shadows, masked in crowds, cautious yet piercing. He was on alert until the second Jack Daniels settled in his gut and his vision adjusted to the dim light of the bar.

About a dozen men, playing pool, drinking beer and sharing sorrows, slumping in barstools and leaning on round wooden tables, took turns looking Ruby over, pawing her with their minds, wondering how a man like Jake could be so lucky. It was pretty much a white man's bar in a working white man's part of town.

Only a matter of time, thought Jake.

A cowboy with a clean-cut look, worn out white plastic hat and polished black boots, approached the table, pool cue in hand.

"M'am," he said, "would you like to play?"

Ruby liked to play and didn't need to be asked twice.

"Rack 'em up, cowboy," she replied. "I'll break."

Crack! The sound of billiard balls in random collision rang in the caverns of Jake's brain. Ruby damn near ran the table and finished the route on her second try.

"This time, I break," said the cowboy.

He sunk two on the break and went on a run of his own. The game was on and the two of them got down to some serious pool.

A man at the bar with the markings of a Mescalero Apache – bola, turquoise and tan moccasins – caught Jake's eye with a few pointed glances before wandering over to introduce himself.

"Don't I know you?" he inquired.

Gazing through whiskey vision, Jake failed to find a glimmer of recognition and wondered what was up. This was not the kind of place where you ran into someone from the reservations. The man was pushing the limits of chance.

"Nice move, mestizo!" the man smiled.

Jake laughed and remembered the three Apaches who witnessed his defense of Ruby's honor in an Arizona motorcycle bar. This man was one of them. It seemed a million miles and a hundred years away. What were the odds?

"What brings you to St. Louis?" asked Jake.

"A job," said the man and from the looks of it he wasn't lying. You can always tell when a typical man lies. He looks down or away and this man did neither. He offered his palm for a firm handshake and took a seat across from Jake.

"The name's Wiley," he said.

"Like the coyote?"

The man nodded and smiled like a coyote.

What were the odds?

A crowd gathered at the pool table where Ruby was

prepared to make a behind the back bank shot. A collective cheer was followed by a groan as first the eight ball dropped and then the cue ball slid into a corner pocket.

"Shit," said Ruby to a round of laughter. Money changed hands as Ruby returned to their table, followed by the victorious cowboy.

"This is Cowboy Bob," said Ruby. "He's alright."

"This is Wiley," introduced Jake. "From Arizona."

"No shit," said Ruby. "Small world."

Ruby gave Jake a warm kiss, whispering that they were going out back for a smoke and wondering if he would like to join them. Jake shook his head and watched the two of them slide out the back.

"Pretty woman," said Wiley.

What were the odds?

Wiley ordered a pitcher of beer and rambled on about life on the Rez, the Apache tradition and the suffering of the people under two centuries of white man rule. He offered tributes to Red Sleeves, Cochise, Geronimo, Marcos and Gomez and lamented the absence of contemporary native leaders.

Jake nodded in agreement with Wiley's sentiments though he held out hope for many contemporary leaders, like Ward Churchill, Leonard Crow Dog, Leonard Peltier behind bars in a Kansas penitentiary and lesser-known tribal leaders like White Wolf. There were many great tribal leaders but few with a platform to air their grievances or inspire their peoples.

"There's one thing I need to ask you," said Wiley, his eyes narrowing to reveal a glimpse of his duplicity. "How is it you follow a white woman?"

Jake sprang to his feet and ran to the rear exit where

the light of day nearly blinded him. He waited for his vision to clear before he found what he already knew: Ruby and the cowboy were nowhere in sight. He walked back into the bar where the coyote was no longer.

It was not the first time he had felt the sting of native betrayal. He left home some time after a man he called a friend seduced his woman with a promise of adventure. The ghost of her madness would never stop haunting him. The sight of her still, lifeless body on the side of the road, twenty paces from his and the burning remains of an old Apache motorcycle, was burned into his mind. It clung to him like Louisiana sweat. He wanted to kill or die but he roamed the land instead.

The bartender wore a quizzical look but said nothing. Jake ordered a whiskey and promptly hurled it against the wall where it shattered and bled. No one moved. No one said a word.

"I'll never drink again," he said to no one but himself.

He did the only thing he could think to do. He went back to the motel and fell into a deep, deep sleep.

There was something about that cowboy's drawl – not Texan, not western but sticky and slow like Louisiana molasses. No wonder Ruby was drawn to him. He was pulling her to her destiny in New Orleans.

Ruby was no longer a Vegas babe or a woman on the run. She was a prize, a jewel, a treasure to be claimed and bartered. The New Orleans mob was in on the hunt.

It was a classic Apache double cross. Like the scouts that tracked down Geronimo, the coyote was hired by the Vegas mob to track down an Indian brother but somewhere along the path, he found Cowboy Bob and made a better deal.

Jake felt it in his bones and saw it in his dream vision: Mississippi black.   Ruby was where she intended to be: On the Mississippi Queen bound for the Easy. She was there but she was no longer in her skin. She was possessed and she was losing hold of everything that made her Ruby Daulton: her freedom, her untamed spirit, and her singular soul.

Jake fell like a stone in black water, deeper and deeper asleep.

EXTERIOR – MOONLIT WATERS OF THE MISSISSIPPI – NIGHT

We see the muddy moonlit waters of the Mississippi River as the Mississippi Queen, a floating paddleboat casino, rolls into view. We hear the voice of Jim Morrison singing CRYSTAL SHIP.

> *Before you slip into unconsciousness*
> *I'd like to have another kiss*
> *Another flashing chance at bliss*
> *Another kiss, another kiss*
>
> *The days are bright and filled with pain*
> *Enclose me in your gentle rain*
> *The time you ran was too insane*
> *We'll meet again, we'll meet again*

INTERIOR – MISSISSIPPI QUEEN – NIGHT

We hear the sounds of drunken gamblers, slot

machines and revelry. We see RUBY in a daze on a red velvet sofa.

> *Oh tell me where your freedom lies*
> *The streets are fields that never die*
> *Deliver me from reasons why*
> *You'd rather cry, Id rather fly*
>
> *The crystal ship is being filled*
> *A thousand girls, a thousand thrills*
> *A million ways to spend your time*
> *When we get back, Ill drop a line*

Fade CRYSTAL SHIP. Fade to black.

SCENE 17: A STONE IN BLACK WATER

FADE IN:

EXTERIOR – MOONLIT WATERS – NIGHT

We sink to the bottom of the moonlit waters of the Mississippi as the Mississippi Queen floats above.

INTERIOR – MISSISSIPPI QUEEN – NIGHT

Fade in the sweet voice of Ruby Daulton singing Billie Holiday's DON'T EXPLAIN.

> *Hush now, don't explain*
> *Just say you'll remain*
> *I'm glad your back, don't explain*

We see a forlorn Ruby, drooping and hazy eyed, at a microphone in the plush, red velvet players' room on the Queen.

> *You know that I love you*
> *And what endures*
> *All my thoughts of you*
> *For I'm so completely yours*

Hush now, don't explain

Pan to faces in the room, men and women, all eyes trained to Ruby with desire and admiration. Gambling and drinking and all activities seem to stop.

CLOSE UP of a handsome, dark complexion man, 45, as a tear rolls down his face. This is the MARQUIS. Fade DON'T EXPLAIN. Fade in GIRL by The Beatles.

> *Is there anybody going to listen to my story*
> *All about the girl who came to stay?*
> *She's the kind of girl you want so much*
> *It makes you sorry*
> *Still you don't regret a single day*
>
> *Ah girl*

Fade to black.

....

Aboard the Mississippi Queen, the war did not exist, the heat was not oppressive, a storm was not brewing in the Tropic of Capricorn, and the poor were only shadows that never reached the light.

Inside the Queen, Darfur, Guantanamo Bay, Fallujah and Abu Ghraib were only words, foreign and far, far away, devoid of terror or loss.

Inside the Queen, no one was destitute, diseased or dying. No one was down on their luck or desperate. No one was betrayed. No one was buried in self-pity. No one cried out in pain. No one absorbed the suffering of the common masses. No one was lost or abandoned except Ruby Daulton.

Ruby was the Queen of the royal court and the Queen was swimming in darkness, descending a spiral staircase into the black waters of the Mississippi where neither man nor beast ever returned.

Ruby would not go gently into that goodnight. She would claw, scratch, tear, bite and fight with every particle of her soulful being. No one takes Ruby down without wearing the wounds of battle.

When Ruby was a child, she was a magnet for the taunts of hungry little boys and jealous little girls until she learned to fight back. What she lacked in technique she made up for in raw passion and she never looked back.

Jake Jones walked onto the Queen decked out in a gray-blue zoot suit tailored for someone of his approximate size and stature. He was a man among boys and he was itching for a fight. He could feel Ruby's light through miles of liquid darkness. He could feel her breath on his neck, her breasts on his chest, her motor revving, her vacuum pulling him in, her song drowning, sinking like a stone in black water.

He strode seamlessly onto the casino floor and the machines began to sing. The anarchy of sound peeled away, revealing the nature and quality of each instrument. The journey had fine-tuned his senses, unraveling the mystery of random chance.

He stepped up to a quarter slot machine to test his theory. Three riverboat queens rolled into perfect alignment: Jackpot.

He was acutely aware of the principle of fallibility. He was not the same man he was in Vegas. Back then there was nothing to lose. Now, he had everything to

lose. Knowing how desire colors the senses, he
struggled to hold back his yearning. A man does not
mold the world to his will but behaves in a manner that
allows the things he needs to come to him. Focusing
too much on the result will lead you to the door but
lose the key.

He noticed the glances of those around him and
realized they had already marked him for a lucky man.
It was too soon to be noticed. He would have to be
shrewd. He thought of Ruby and played it cool. Lose a
little; win a lot. Lose a little more; win again.

He felt the great river rushing beneath his feet. It
gave him strength and bolstered his confidence and at
the same time he felt its power for good and ill.

A woman on a poker machine three rows down and
to his left gathered her tokens and walked away just as
the machine began to sing. He tipped the roaming
waitress and made his way to the machine in question.
Five quarters hit a full house. Five more pulled four
sevens. Five more drew a straight flush. Five more
pulled an Ace, King, Jack, Ten of Hearts and a Queen of
Spades. He did not hesitate. He discarded the black
Queen and drew a ruby red Queen of Hearts: Royal
Flush.

Jake Jones had been noticed.

In the corner of his eye, he saw him. At the top of
the stairs on the far end of the floor, in a dark blue suit
with a slick white New Orleans jazz hat, the figure of
an Indian stood smiling, glaring, challenging. The
Coyote was onboard.

Behind the door at the top of the stairs, in a room
reserved for players, propped up by two large black
escorts and surrounded by red velvet, Ruby took the

stage. She felt herself losing hold of the world around her, losing touch with her own senses, losing grasp of a law governed reality, losing connection with the solid ground of earth.

She remembered an old song, so long ago, so far removed from here and now, when nothing seemed to matter and nothing but the moment was important. Ruby sang:

Hush now, don't explain

The world had turned to liquid before her eyes, slowly drifting by, light and color bleeding and separating in an endless parade, pulsing and falling in harmony beyond her reach. Ruby sang:

Quiet, don't explain

She fell to the bottom of the deep dark sea and lived in a liquid slow motion reality, motionless and still, watching the procession of life around her. Ruby sang:

Cry to hear folks chatter
And I know you cheat
Right or wrong, don't matter
When you're with me, sweet

She felt no pain, no sorrow, no worries. She had no fear. Like a snail with its feelers extending outward from her shell, she was helpless and completely vulnerable. Ruby sang:

Hush now, don't explain
You're my joy and pain

My life's yours love
Don't explain

When Ruby sang, every angel in heaven and every sentient soul on earth wept a river of tears and the black waters of the Mississippi rolled on.

She was no longer Ruby Daulton, Queen of Hearts; she was a kept thing like a poodle and she did not care. Her masters would care for her, tell her what a pretty thing she was, stroke her, kiss and caress her. She belonged to them and she did not care.

Jake heard her voice from behind the doors at the top of the stairs and his heart stopped. He collected his bearings and his winnings before approaching the men guarding the doors.

"How much to play?" he asked.

"We're very pleased you inquired," said a man. "We require an account of twenty thousand."

He produced his winnings in a tidy stack of black and gold chips. The man smiled, took his name and two gold chips for deposit.

Out of the darkness, out of the swirling lights and sound, out of the symphony of rumbling, roaring electrons, out of the depths of a bottomless pit where sirens sing and spirits dance on flames of desire, two words sprang forth like a beacon from a lighthouse on a jagged shore.

"Mr. Jake Jones," announced the doorman.

A man in dark, shoulder length hair, impeccably dressed in the latest Parisian suit, looked up, his olive face registering surprise, and said, "Show him in."

The Coyote stood glaring from the shadows across the room and Ruby, now seated in a velvet corner, was far gone from the world of light. Her eyes rolled back and she swooned before collapsing on a lush pillowed sofa, the hint of smile on her pale white face.

"Allow me to introduce myself," said the man in the Parisian suit. "I am the Marquis and I assure you, she is in no danger."

Jake betrayed no fear. He had found his adversary and the game was on.

"You like to play games of chance?" asked the Marquis.

"There's no such thing as chance," Jake replied.

The Marquis smiled and introduced the players. They were not the Vegas crowd, the hard-edged hustlers that taught Ruby to play. By all appearances (and in this case appearances were not deceptive), they were southern gentry. They could afford to lose and the one vice they shared above all others was pride.

The game was Texas hold-em and the limit was the house but, by gentleman's agreement, they would allow Jake to either stake his position or yield his seat before they went for the kill. Nothing was said. No agreement was struck. It was understood.

The cards were from the Vegas Mirage, informing Jake that Guido Lazerri was connected here. The Marquis, who alone pushed the conversation forward, took note.

"You find our choice of playing cards of interest?" he asked.

Jake remained silent, preferring to focus on the players as waitresses dressed for distraction served drinks of choice. He chose a glass of ice tea. He could not help but wonder if the game was rigged but dismissed the notion. The Marquis was as honorable as a man in his position could afford to be. He was by all appearances the consummate professional.

"We share acquaintances at the Mirage," said the Marquis. "And we have common interests," he added with a glance at Ruby who was now sinking in liquid darkness, incapable of recognizing that her hero had arrived.

"An Italian gentleman," he went on as the first hand was dealt. "Though the term should be reserved for the gentile," he smiled. "Indeed, it was not long ago that he sat where you sit now. In fact, it seems like only yesterday."

The Marquis threw in on the third round of betting. Jake bumped on a pair of Jacks and the others folded. Within a half dozen hands, he built a nice stack and the two of them were securing their positions. The Marquis was established as a player who knew the odds and could not be pushed around. Jake was feeling him out.

"The Italian had a particular attraction to the ladies," said the Marquis between hands. "It was an obvious flaw in his game. I warned him it would be his downfall but he did not understand my language."

The dealer dealt two down and bets were placed. Two threw in, leaving three along with Jake on the small blind and the Marquis. The turn laid out a queen of hearts, jack of spades and an ace of diamonds. Everyone stayed in until the Marquis doubled the pot.

Jake placed his hand on his down cards without looking. His eyes peered into the Marquis' eyes, eyes that held the cold darkness of a Mississippi grave. What he saw there, in that impenetrable depth, in that layered mystery of fog and mist, had no words but it betrayed a particle of doubt.

Every poker game comes down to two players. The game is a process of discovering who those players are. Once the discovery is made it becomes a question of which will prevail. Only one can win; the other will lose. Everyone else is just holding a seat.

At this table, on this evening, as the Queen rolled down the great river, as Ruby swam in the murky depths, it came down to Jake and the Marquis. Jake was the challenger. His greatest asset was that he was unknown and unknowable to those who graced the player's table in the velvet room on the Mississippi Queen. The more they watched, the less they saw. They more confident they grew, the less they understood.

Only the Marquis knew what drove him though he did not fully appreciate how far he would go to achieve his objective, to free his beloved Ruby. In time, he would understand completely. Jake was the kind of man he rarely encountered and invariably underestimated.

Jake called and the others politely folded. The Marquis glanced at his cards, at Jake's remaining chips and signaled the dealer to play on.

Fourth Street was a jack of hearts. The Marquis asked for a chip count and forced Jake all in with a raise.

Fifth Street was a ten of hearts. The Marquis deferred to Jake and Jake asked for house rules on betting beyond one's holdings.

"What would you like to bet?" asked the Marquis.

"All that I have, my life and my name, for Ruby."

The Marquis smiled. Until this moment, he had

Jake pegged as a loser: the noble hero who rushes headlong into a hopeless situation, the character who always prevails in fairy tales and formula Hollywood movies but stands no chance against the hardcore realities of life.

Now he saw another side of Jake Jones: a gambler who made careful calculations and took his best shot. Now he understood that if he were in Jake's shoes he might well make the same calculations and arrive at the same conclusion: This was the shot.

Narrowed down to a simple fact: He admired Jake and somewhere in the long forgotten chambers of his mind where romance still found a home, he wanted Jake to win. By that acknowledgement alone, Jake had already won.

"Gentlemen," said the Marquis, "we are pleased to witness a rare phenomenon. Here is a man who understands that we are not engaged in a game of chance. We are summoning forces beyond light and beyond darkness, beyond life and death. We are reaching for the gods and risking our souls.

"Unfortunately, Mr. Jones, I am not in a position to accept your wager. The lady is not mine to gamble. However, you may wager any monetary amount you choose. Your honor is beyond question and your credit is good."

Jake declined the offer and let the bet stand. He had no real concept of how much money was represented except that it was a large amount.

The Marquis turned over an ace and a queen of spades. Jake revealed his destiny with Ruby Daulton: an ace and a queen of hearts for a royal flush.

"Congratulations," said the Marquis. "Will you be

playing on?"

Jake shook his head and rose, not knowing where he would go or what he would do next. He heard the word "burgundy" and saw an image of Ruby swallowed in darkness, eyes fluttering from side to side, as if observing a carousel, yet she remained absolutely still, her mind severed from her body, limp yet warm like jelly in a plastic bag.

He awakened in a Memphis hotel alone.

> *Bang! Bang! Maxwell's silver hammer*
> *Came down upon his head*
> *Bang! Bang! Maxwell's silver hammer*
> *Made sure that he was...*

> *Number nine, number nine, number nine...*

SCENE 18: DREAMLAND

FADE IN:

EXTERIOR – LIQUID DREAMSCAPE – NIGHT

Ruby sinks in liquid darkness, naked and unafraid, as the voice of John Lennon sings (HOW from *Imagine*).

> *How can I go forward when I don't know*
> *Which way I'm facing?*
> *How can I go forward when I don't know*
> *Which way to turn?*
> *How can I go forward into something I'm not sure of?*
> *Oh no, oh no…*

INTERIOR – MEMPHIS HOTEL ROOM – NIGHT

Jake sleeps motionless and fully clothed in his gambling attire. An unopened briefcase sits on a desk. CLOSE UP of Jake's face as his eyes flash open in horror yet he remains motionless.

> *You know life can be long and you got to be so strong*
> *And the world, she is tough*
> *Sometimes I feel I've had enough*

How can we go forward when we don't know
Which way we're facing?
How can we go forward when we don't know
Which way to turn?
How can we go forward into something we're not sure of?
Oh no, oh no…

. . . .

When everything around you is sinking and you are sinking with everything around you, it appears that everything is motionless, still life, a photograph, no life, death.

When all around you has turned to liquid and you can no longer feel your arms, your legs, the beating of your heart, you realize you are no longer distinct from the surrounding darkness. You are the darkness, the liquid darkness, and you are still yet you are falling, sinking, losing hold of the solid earth that once held you together and kept you apart from the darkness that enfolds everything it touches.

Ruby was sinking and she could no longer care. Ruby was dying and she could no longer remember why it was she needed to fight back. Her mother was a liquid memory, less real than unreal, her father was a whisper in the night, and Jake – Jake was a man she never knew but only imagined in a summer daydream.

The only thing she could hold onto that tied her to the world she once knew and the dreams she once dreamed was the music she carried in her soul. Lost in this dreamland of endless void, Ruby had a song to sing and she sang as if everything she knew and felt, loved and hated depended on it. Ruby sang the blues and a river of infinite sorrow flowed from the depths of creation.

Ruby sang songs she never knew she knew with a depth and clarity few in this world or the next can ever attain. Ruby sang the blues from the canons of Etta James, T-Bone Walker, Ella Fitzgerald, Janis Joplin, Bessie Smith and the immortal Billie Holliday: *My Man, Strange Fruit, Don't Explain, Ball and Chain, God Bless the Child, Stormy Monday, Cry Me a River...* Ruby sang the blues and everyman and everywoman prayed for her salvation, as if they understood as they never understood before that their salvation was chained to Ruby's salvation. They understood as they never understood before that once the pure of heart fell, it would all come crashing down, like a dam breaking or a river run wild, leaving no one unscathed.

No one gets out alive.

They understood that Ruby was the collective soul of the innocent and pure yet they could only bear witness and cry and pray. They could only share some piece of her suffering and hope by the act of contrition and empathy they could somehow ease her pain. Maybe they could.

Jake heard Ruby sing from the depths of his mad slumber. He awakened long enough to take account and surmise what had happened. He found a briefcase full of cash, large denominations, and a note:

Would you dance with the devil, Mr. Jones? What would you offer a man who has no needs? Let the full weight of this proposition settle before you venture forth.

Let no man say the Marquis does not pay his debts.

Jake had been drugged and he cursed himself for

allowing it to happen. Now he felt the sleeping disease creeping through his veins: systemic paralysis. He managed to call the desk and delivered five hundred in cash with the explanation that he did not know how many days he would stay.

He laid down on the bed and let go of the world. He would have to rely on second sight. He would have to use the gift of spirit flight that White Wolf revealed to him so many moons ago when he was struggling to cope with his disorder.

He closed his eyes and let it all go. He felt his spirit rise and saw himself prone, motionless on the hotel bed. He let it go and saw the rusted, sprawling city of Memphis and the great river. He let it go and soared like the hawk that lived within him. He followed the river coursing through the great forest until he came to the giant paddleboat, the floating casino, the Riverboat Queen that held his heart captive and held his love in bondage.

Preparing for a world in which he had only eyes and could not act, he let go and boarded the Queen just miles outside the Port of New Orleans.

From the moment she arrived, even through the surreal vision of a drug-induced haze, Ruby knew she had come home. She was once a Vegas girl but that was only a façade, a sequined costume, a veil of glamour, an artificial reflection of the real thing. New Orleans was Ruby's soul and Ruby was New Orleans.

New Orleans is a city of destiny. Without adding it up, Ruby knew it was number nine. Doomed by its geography and the willful neglect of government to defend her, New Orleans was the sacred womb of the nation and the sweetest, most enchanting of lovers:

The birthplace of jazz, a culture of tolerance that predates the nation, Bourbon Street, Jackson Square, the St. Louis Cemetery and the tomb of Marie Laveaux, a city of a million contradictions and mysteries, city of light and darkness, city of hope and despair, city of faith and godlessness, city of passion and unholy calm, city of blues, Creole, Zydeco, ragtime and jazz. More than anything else it is the city of jazz.

It is a city that pulls at the heartstrings and permeates the souls of all it claims. It haunts them like a mother's love, like a lover's cry, like a full moon on an endless night. Wherever the people that belonged to her went, whatever they did, New Orleans followed them, crept inside of them, calling to them: Come home.

Ruby was home.

Here, despite the ominous presence of the nation's dark intelligence community, there was no war and politics was only an afterthought. The city belonged to the music that defined her and set her apart from every other city on earth. She was the queen, she was the heart, she was the womb and the soul of the nation.

Everyone in New Orleans seemed to be waiting: waiting for sunset, waiting for Bourbon Street to come alive with music, dance and revelry, waiting for a summer storm that hung in the thick, palpable air like an omen of doom.

You could see it in the eyes of those who walked her streets: an indefinable feeling of desperation, a yearning, and a sense of loss. Something was terribly wrong. That sense of destiny that so often gave them comfort through hard times now offered only a warning: Get out while you can. Their lives were balanced on a thread and they knew it in their bones.

It left them paralyzed for there was no place to go. They belonged to New Orleans. Like jazz, itself, they could never be at home anywhere else. They could never be at peace anywhere but in the Big Easy.

New Orleans was Ruby Daulton and Ruby was New Orleans. Jazz, dancing women, black magic, gambling, an air of mystery and a taste of death, Ruby was the liquid sky and the distant stars. She was the dream they dreamed and the lover they longed to meet.

She was escorted from the Queen to the palatial estate of Louie Marchant in the heart of the French Quarters on Burgandy Street. Bought and sold like the mulatto descendants of slaves in a former era, Ruby would become the plaything of a man who fancied himself a duke, lord and protectorate of the House of Burgandy.

He was known as "Pale Louie" for the absence of color in his skin and his habit of never emerging in daylight. His estate ran deep into the bosom of the infamous New Orleans underground and it was there, in a dark expansive and luxuriously decorated space, that he kept his collection of pale-skinned beauties. It was there in that foreboding space that he entertained the royalty and courtesans of the underground through the long, cold nights of winter and the hot, sweltering nights of summer.

From the moment he heard Ruby sing, he knew she was special. She would be a kept woman, a slave to his desires, but no one would be allowed to violate her body or her spirit. She alone would be off limits to his clientele. She alone would be protected as long as he breathed. He would grant her every wish. He would provide her with the most exquisite jewelry, the most elite gowns, the best cuisine and finest wine. He would give her everything she desired save freedom. She would become a legend in the underground but she could never leave. She could never walk outside its gates a free woman.

It was the one condition Guido Lazerri insisted on besides cold cash and one the duke had no reason to refuse: Ruby would never leave New Orleans. From the moment he saw her pale image in a photograph, a hint of danger beneath a veil of innocence, an unattainable beauty and a knowing that reached back through the ages, the duke knew he could never risk losing her. She would remain in his underground kingdom and even on those rare occasions when she would be allowed to walk the streets, to breathe the air of a timeless city, to hear her jazz and feel her rhythm, armed guards would always accompany her.

Ruby could never leave.

So Ruby sang the blues and her tears flowed like a river of sorrow, like the waters that would soon break through the levees of Lake Pontchartrain and the 17th Street Canal, burying the ninth ward and much of the city, implanting in its timeless soul a sorrow that would never lose its hold.

FADE IN:

EXTERIOR – SCENES OF NEW ORLEANS – NIGHT AND DAY

A funeral procession marches through the streets of New Orleans, as stills of Gentilly, the Lower Ninth

Ward, the levees, jazz joints and the Quarters reveal the soul of the Easy before the storm. The procession transitions from mourning to revelry and the city marches on.

We hear and see Ruby on a dark stage, her tear stained face in spotlight. Ruby sings CRY ME A RIVER by Arthur Hamilton.

> *Now you say you're lonely*
> *You cried the long night through*
> *Well, you can cry me a river, cry me a river*
> *I cried a river over you*
>
> *Now you say you're sorry*
> *For being so untrue*
> *Well, you can cry me a river, cry me a river*
> *I cried, cried, cried a river over you*

Fade scene.

SCENE 19: N'ORLEANS

FADE IN:

EXTERIOR – PORT OF NEW ORLEANS – DUSK

Ruby is escorted from the Mississippi Queen by armed guards, accompanied by the Marquis. We hear Ruby singing W.C. Handy's SAINT LOUIS BLUES.

I hate to see that evening sun go down
Lord, I hate to see that evening sun go down
Cause my baby he done left this town

INTERIOR – LOUIE'S UNDERGROUND – NIGHT

We see a sleepy-eyed Ruby standing at a microphone, pale-skinned beauties all around, smoking opium, sharing stories and entertaining the gentlemen of the New Orleans underground.

Feeling tomorrow like I feel today
Feeling tomorrow like I feel today
I'm gonna pack my bags and make my getaway

CLOSE UP of a man in the balcony with pale white skin, his face marked in the agony of desire. This is

PALE LOUIE, 45.   We hear the voice of John Lennon
singing I WANT YOU (SHE'S SO HEAVY).

> *I want you*
> *I want you so bad*
> *I want you*
> *I want you so bad*
> *It's driving me mad, it's driving me mad*

....

To the elder caretaker of the old section of Saint
Louis Cemetery, the shadowy figure of Louie Marchant
was a familiar sight.   He always appeared after dusk,
always following the same course through the elevated
tombs and burial plots, always pausing in the same
spots, particularly at the elaborate gravesite of the
House of Burgandy where he would someday take his
final repose.

Shrouded in darkness, black flowing hair and cape
contrasting with his pale white face, he stood
transfixed, as if imaging a family history that ran
parallel to the history of New Orleans itself. At length,
the spell was broken by an expansive sigh as he
continued his evening stroll through Louis Armstrong
Park into the dark back alleyways of Vieux Carre,
emerging with the bustling, jazz filled, alcohol and sex
driven crowds on Bourbon Street.

Virtually anywhere else, the mere appearance of
Pale Louie – as he was known to the locals – with his
shroud of darkness, piercing black eyes and gossamer
skin, would draw all eyes but in the French Quarters on
a sultry summer night, with the first winds of a storm

drawing in from the Gulf, Louie blended seamlessly into the mix.

No one who knew him or knew anything about him dared approach Louie without an invitation. Not even the Voodoo Queens of Lafayette or Metairie doubted the powers of the dark prince in the heart of the Quarters. Stories of those who crossed him, even by some meaningless gesture or involuntary expression, were countless, invariably ending with a bloodless corpse in the marshlands of Lake Pontchartrain.

In a world of infinite possibilities and random chance, if there were such a thing as vampires, Louie would have been their ancient king. As it was, he cultivated the image, savored it and refused to deny persistent rumors that he had on numerous occasions dined on human blood.

None but a madman or saint, if there were such a thing as sainthood, would ever follow Louie within the confines of his dark realm but someone was following him now. So subtle and discrete was he, so soft were his footsteps that Louie himself was only vaguely aware of being observed. He turned once at the corner of Saint Louis and again at the corner of Dauphine but he saw nothing – only the usual wide-eyed tourists looking for the kind of action and adventure that one could only find in the Quarters.

Below the crimson glow of balcony lights, their voices swallowed by a strange hybrid of Zydeco, Cajun and Dixieland jazz, the drunken, drug-infested swarm moved as an interconnected mass, a serpent of desire oblivious to all below the surface of their own desperate libidos.

Louie turned one last time and closely surveyed

what remained of the Bourbon Street swarm: a stumbling, pot-bellied Cajun, a Creole drag queen, a peddler of voodoo trinkets, and the fleeting shadow of a man in a jazz hat and a square-shouldered suit.

As if puzzled by a phenomenon he had never before experienced, Louie sighed and let it go. He had other pressing business. The Mississippi Queen would dock shortly at the Port of New Orleans and it carried a valuable cargo and a very special guest.

He marked a course at a quickened pace down the back alleys until he reached what appeared to be a storage shed, where what appeared to be a couple of derelicts sprang to their feet, unlatched and opened the doors, revealing a descending stairwell to the Burgandy underground.

The Queen docked ahead of schedule but was delayed by a small army of port inspectors on a mission. Ostensibly, they were conducting the public business, protecting the citizenry from the scourge of illicit goods. In reality, they were raising private funds for a looming storm.

New Orleans had always existed on borrowed time. In the second coming of the age of privatization, the delicate marshes that had long protected the city, refurbishing sunken land with fresh topsoil, diffusing the force of storms from the gulf, were allowed to erode and fall to encroaching waters. Marshes were of little use to oil refineries, chemical plants and land developers until the next big hurricane intensified over the warm waters of the Gulf of Mexico and threatened all in its path with catastrophic destruction.

As global climate patterns changed, driven by melting glaciers, exacerbated by diminishing ozone, caused by a massive accumulation of toxic carbon dioxide in the atmosphere, oceanic currents changed with them. Those who struggled to make a living fishing the waters off the Gulf Coast grew more despondent every year as the red tides became more destructive, the wildlife diminished and the waters themselves grew warmer and warmer.

Everyone on the coast knew it was only a matter of time. The levees erected after the flood of 1913 to protect the sinking lowlands, where poor black folks were allowed to buy homes and establish businesses – Gentilly, St. Bernard Parish, the Ninth Ward – were decades too old and badly in need of massive overhaul. It was said they might stand up to a category three storm but they would never hold up against the big one.

The lead inspector of the Port Authority crew summoned the ship's captain and the Marquis into the captain's quarters for negotiations. The conversation opened as all conversations in New Orleans opened these days.

"Storm's coming in. Could be the big one."

"That's what they always say," said the captain.

"The gypsy down at Marie Laveau's says it is and she aint often wrong," replied the inspector.

The Marquis saw fear in the inspector's eyes and knew better than to toy with him. The Queen was an institution supplying the illicit needs of New Orleans, Memphis, Nashville, Saint Louis, Kansas City, Chicago and Detroit according the law of supply and demand. In more than a decade of interplay with the chief inspector of the Port of New Orleans, he had never witnessed a whisper of fear before.

"What can we do for you?" asked the Marquis.

"We're asking a one time contingency fee," said the inspector. "Double the usual price."

"Done," said the Marquis, "and I'll double that out of my own treasure."

The Marquis knew the value of trust in New Orleans and trust in a time of crisis came at a premium. Trust in New Orleans was as good as blood and blood was everything. To the Marquis it was an investment and a commitment to the community. It was as prudent and wise an investment as he would ever make.

The inspector nodded with such humility that the captain almost blushed. Hands were clasped and hugs embraced before the money changed hands. To the Marquis, it was worth every red cent and Louie need never know. From this moment forward, the inspector would answer to him first.

"Word to the wise," said the inspector in parting, "get the Queen out of here first light. This aint no easy ride coming."

The Marquis thanked him and the inspector departed a contented man. Whatever the future held, he would have the resources to take care of his own. It was all he could ask and he would carry the debt proudly.

A warm wind brought a warm rain to the Quarters as Louie's entourage arrived at the port and the prized jewel of New Orleans was given a queen's escort to the House of Burgandy where Pale Louie awaited.

Ruby was adorned in costume, jewelry and makeup before she was delivered to the stage of Louie's underground nightclub. She did not need to be told

what to do.
   Ruby sang.

> *I hate to see that evening sun go down*
> *Lord, I hate to see that evening sun go down*
> *Cause my sweet darling, he's gone and left this town*

Ruby sang and ripped the heart of New Orleans from its warm and tender womb.

SCENE 20: BONES AND THE MONK

FADE IN:

INTERIOR – BURGANDY UNDERGROUND – NIGHT

A hazy-eyed Ruby on stage, clinging to a mike stand, sings a song never before heard, slow and sultry: TUESDAY BLUE.

> *Sunday premonition in the air, it's everywhere*
> *Monday intuition and I'm wishing not to care*
> *Come Tuesday, I'll be blue once again, my sad friend*
> *Lord, I'll be Tuesday blue 'til the end*

INTERIOR – GREYHOUND BUS – DAY

Day turns to night as Jake gazes out the window of a Greyhound Bus heading south in a deep forest. He seems entranced, distracted, as if in a dream state.

INTERIOR – BURGANDY UNDERGROUND – NIGHT

Ruby sings.

> *Now they're saying I don't care Lord*
> *I don't think they're being fair*

Well, I'll leave it up to you Lord
For better or for worse
It's not that I don't care Lord
I do but I come first

CLOSE UP of Ruby's tears as she struggles to remember loves lost.

EXTERIOR – ATLANTIC OCEAN, ARIEL VIEW – DUSK

A hurricane grows stronger as it courses west across the Atlantic toward the Yucatan, Cuba and the Gulf of Mexico.

Number nine, number nine, number nine...

....

The rain came down like a runaway train and the skies stayed black all day, as if the sun was mourning, as if the sky could no longer hold its heavy burden. The rain came down, pounding the sidewalks, the cobbled roads and awnings overlooking storefronts and sidewalk cafes like drummers on a funeral march.

Jake deposited his bags in locker number 99, picked up an umbrella on the first corner and began walking every street and alley in and around the French Quarters. He located the alley where Pale Louie made his hidden descent and struck up a drunken conversation with the boys protecting the gateway. They were nervous and stone cold sober but not unfriendly.

He made a taxicab tour of the pump stations along

the Industrial, 17th Street and London Avenue canals. All of them were underground, which did not bode well for a flood, but the Burgandy House underground could be reached through any of them if a man knew the way.

Everyone in the Quarters could be influenced by a bottle of whiskey and bought for the right amount of cash so Jake brought plenty of both wherever he went. A pump worker in Plaquemines Parrish sold him a sketched map of the water and sewer lines. A gypsy woman in Gentilly sold him her blessings. The cabbie sold him the name and location of a man in the Ninth Ward who could answer all his needs: a safe house, local connections and local knowledge.

As they pulled up at the bar where the Monk did business, the cabbie gave Jake a word of warning: "I like you, Mr. Jones. I like doing business with you. Like to do more of it. Everyone here has an affinity for the natives around here. Feel a connection. But they got a way of treating newcomers no matter what they skin color. You give him this card and tell him Bones sent you."

Jake looked at the card: A simple black-and-white skull and crossbones.

"One more thing. Monk will sell you what you want but you got to know: There's a powerful storm coming in. We all know. Feel it in our blood. Going to make Betsy and Camille seem like child's play. Not a real good time to be buying a house...or maybe it is. Just so you know."

Jake thanked him and stepped from the cab where two large black men at the door of the bar looked him over, sniffing him like a dog to sense if there was fear in his heart or treachery in his soul.

"I'll wait here for about twenty minutes. You don't come out by then, you're on your own," said the cabbie.

Jake approached the doormen and asked to see the Monk.

"What's your business?"

"Real estate."

The men paused, laughed and looked around for any unmarked cop cars or unknown bystanders.

"You got a weapon?"

Jake unstrapped his knife and handed it to the man who did the talking.

"Anything else?"

Jake had the foresight to leave Ruby's derringer back at the locker. He raised his arms and allowed the silent one to pat him down.

They stepped aside and Jake walked in, followed by the talking man. He waited by the door for his eyes to adjust to bar light while the man walked to a back corner table, leaned over and whispered to a well-dressed man with a gray suit and a slick gray jazz hat. Like an owl in moonlight, Monk found Jake's eyes and drilled into them like a surgeon with a scalpel.

The talking man delivered a message: "The Monk aint doing business today. Come back tomorrow."

"I don't have time," said Jake as he reached into his pocket and pulled out a wad of bills, handing it to the messenger.

The talking man waved the bills in the air and glanced back at the Monk who pretended not to notice.

"This is good," said the man. "It'll get you in the door tomorrow."

"I don't have time," said Jake.

"I aint going to tell you again."

He waited, smiled, shook his head and walked to the bar as another man, a black man with all the signs of a seasoned prize fighter, puffy eyes, cauliflower ears and a broad flattened nose, walked out of the shadows as if on cue.

"They a problem here?"

"I don't have time."

"The Monk done spoke," said the fighter. "The only choice you got, mister, is whether you going to leave standing or the other way."

"I don't have time."

The fighter threw a punch quicker than a coiled snake but Jake caught it and deflected it away from its target.

Jake lowered his center as the fighter circled, throwing soft jabs to test his opponent's reactions, and circling back with harder shots that Jake easily deflected. The bartender let a bottle of beer drop to the floor as the fighter unleashed a torrid combination ending with a right cross that caught Jake square on the jaw, sending him stumbling back.

The fighter closed in for a knock out but Jake felt his breath, his pulse, his approaching heartbeat, and planted an elbow in his gut, spinning and connecting his heel to the fighter's jaw. The blow would have knocked down a horse but the fighter kept his feet beneath him as he wobbled back and back and back.

Anger flared in his eyes as he finally moved forward but the talking man intervened, placing himself between Jake and the raging bull.

"That's enough."

The fighter looked back to the Monk who nodded and he returned to his appointed seat where a couple of fine looking women bathed him with tender affection.

"Monk will see you now," said the man.

Jake took a breath and walked over to the corner table where Monk did not look up from his accounts before he spoke.

"Never seen anyone put the fear in Beau outside the ring. You a fighter?"

"I'm a ghost," replied Jake. "Kachina magic."

Monk looked up with a broad smile, exposing a full set of perfect, pearly white teeth.

"Anywhere else they'd mark you a fool. Around here, we got lots of magic."

"Where I come from," replied Jake, "a man without magic has nothing."

"I believe you," said Monk.

Jake placed the card the cabbie gave him on the table.

"Friend of Bones, are you?"

"He sent me here to see you."

"Well, Bones wouldn't send nobody he didn't trust like a brother. What can I do for you, Mr. Jones?"

Jake did not wonder how the Monk knew his name. He would be surprised if he did not know everything Bones knew and maybe a little more. He figured the Monk was not the kind of man you kept in the dark so he decided to lay it all on the line.

He needed a safe house in the Ninth Ward and its numbers had to add to the number nine. He needed nine men and women – at least two women – reliable and trustworthy. He needed a presentable suit and an invitation to the Burgandy underground. He had cash and he was willing to spend whatever it took.

Monk skipped the usual foreplay, called on a woman to bring him a listing for the lower Ninth, called on another to take measurements, and drew up a list of names he handed to a third. He pointed a finger to a listing for a house and circled it.

"There it is, Mr. Jones. As it happens, we got a storm sale going on. Does nine grand sound about right?"

Jake nodded and extended his hand.

"One more thing before we seal this deal. Who's the mark?"

"Pale Louie."

Monk smiled to appreciate the moment. No one had the balls to take on Pale Louie, certainly no one who was in town less than twenty-four hours.

"Some say you can't kill Louie. Others say it aint worth it for all the voodoo curses be hanging around your neck."

"I don't plan to kill him."

"What do you plan to do: Put him to sleep?"

"He has something doesn't belong to him."

"Something or someone?"

"Someone."

"The white woman."

Jake took a step back. How could he know unless he had seen her and if he had, was he connected to the underground? Were they all connected?

"You know about Ruby."

"Shit man, everyone knows about Ruby Daulton."

He snapped his fingers and Ruby's voice filled the bar, singing Bessie's *Backwater Blues* like no one ever did since the late great diva of blues herself.

When it rains five days
And the skies turn dark as night
When it rains five days
And the skies turn dark as night
Then trouble's takin' place in the lowlands at night

"This is a bootleg recording. It's all over town. We all got a soft spot for the lady and some of us know about the man she left behind."

He looked at Jake with renewed interest.

"You the man she be singing about?"

"I plan to get her out," replied Jake.

They shook hands and Monk gave instructions to the talking man to fetch Bones.

"We going to have us a real toast on this deal," he announced.

Ruby sang:

When it thunders and lightning
And the wind begins to blow
When it thunders and lightning
And the wind begins to blow
There's thousands of people aint got no place to go

SCENE 21: NINE O'CLOCK AT BURGANDY

FADE IN:

EXTERIOR – LOWER NINTH WARD – SUNSET

An ominous, dark and infinitely beautiful sunset sky zooms in to the number 927 on the porch column of Jake's newly purchased safe house in the lower ninth ward.

INTERIOR – PRIEUR STREET HOUSE – SUNSET

Holding a shot glass with a green liquid, MONK offers a toast to JAKE, fitted in a classy dark suit, jazz hat and fitted with a fake goatee, for his plot to free RUBY from PALE LOUIE'S underground prison. Two women and seven men, all African American, join them in a circle, as Ruby's bootleg recording plays in the background: Bessie Smith's BACKWATER BLUES.

When it thunders and lightning
And the wind begins to blow

FADE OUT MONK'S BAR, FADE IN:

INTERIOR – BURGANDY UNDERGROUND – NIGHT

RUBY on stage in a pool of light sings.

> *Well it thundered and lightened*
> *And the winds began to blow*
> *Well it thundered and lightened*
> *And the winds began to blow*
> *There was a thousand poor women,*
> *Didn't have no place to go*

Fade scene.

....

    Monk made good on his word and Jake made good on his. Bones took him to the bus station, where he retrieved his bags and a briefcase full of cash, and returned him to his two-story safe house at 927 Prieur Street, where Monk and his people had cleaned and furnished the upstairs, leaving the street floor barren.

    Money was counted and exchanged and Monk introduced six men (Bones was the seventh) and two women who could be counted on to carry out Jake's plan – as long as it did not entail killing Pale Louie – on that they would have no part.

    They were street people, musicians, hustlers and gophers, who got along just fine with a little help from their friend, the Monk. Consequently, they had a sense of loyalty bordering on devotion. If Monk ordered them to kill Pale Louie they would try to talk him out of it but failing that, they would give it their best shot.

    Monk had too much respect for the ways of the underground to give such an order, no matter what the mysterious man was rumored to have done. There was not enough money in New Orleans to order that hit and Louie knew it.

Monk had intimate connections with the N'Orleans underground of which Louie was a central figure. He used them to collect three invitations to the Burgandy House establishment where Ruby Daulton was being hailed as the new voice of the real Big Easy.

Monk provided Jake appropriate attire, a dark jazz funeral-style suit, with a fake goatee to serve as disguise, a couple of escorts in bright red gowns and a Cadillac limousine with Bones as the driver. He was required to appear at the street level entry of Burgandy House precisely at nine o'clock – three minutes later, he would not be admitted. It was Pale Louie's way of keeping a low profile. There would never be a crowd outside his doors.

After a short lull, the rain resumed its pounding, jackhammer beat and the wind swept through the streets like a lost highway on the high plains, alternating from a whistle to a scream, foreshadowing the storm to come.

She had a name now and she was pounding the Yucatan peninsula, triggering mudslides that buried whole villages of poor people who were accustomed to disasters. With nowhere else to go and no one to welcome or assist them, they would build again until the next disaster struck. As always, it would only be a flicker on the nightly television screens of wealthy nations. Maybe the Red Cross would send aid, maybe not. Maybe that assistance would reach the people, more than likely it would not.

They would survive. Help or no help, media focus

or not, they would survive.

Five boys in rubber boots and slickers on the corner of Reynes and Prieur, drenched and huddled against the wall of a neighborhood liquor store, sang with the rhythm of the pounding storm, the words arriving with the wind and the pouring rain.

> *Rain came down like a runaway train*
> *Listen to the pouring rain lord*
> *Listen to the pouring rain*

Jake and his escorts climbed in their limousine at precisely 8:30 and the driver measured his route, pausing at safe locations inside the Quarters, timing their arrival for an appointment with destiny.

> *Plaquemine preacher said a prayer today*
> *Listen to the pouring rain lord*
> *Listen to the pouring rain*

Jake presented his embossed invitations to the doorman and they were immediately directed through an expansive, chandeliered greeting room, furnished in seventeenth century New Orleans with magnificent erotic paintings, sculpture and objects of affection. They followed their escort up a winding wrought iron staircase to an equally lavish waiting room, where they were seated and served cocktails while the eyes of Louie Marchant examined them through the magic of modern surveillance technology.

Louie insisted on personally approving every visitor to the underground, especially now that he possessed the most prized jewel of New Orleans.

Having seen nothing but a fleeting shadow of a

ghost by the name of Jake Jones, Louie had no reason to be alarmed. He and his entourage were typical of the clientele that Monk sent his way. They were always a little out of place, a little under-dressed and less extravagant than the normal crowd, but Louie felt they added texture to the otherwise uniform display of wealth.

The doors of an antique elevator opened, the attendant bowed and welcomed them to the underground. As they entered a cavernous concert hall, its walls lined with blue velvet curtains, its furnishings striking a contrast in carved wood and red velvet against a gray marble floor with gold and red oriental carpets, they were politely asked if they had any weapons and escorted through an x ray machine.

They were shown to a table half back from the stage and off center to the right. The attendant bowed again and refused a hundred dollar tip as an old black sax player in a jazz quartet finished a set inspired by John Coltrane and Ornette Coleman.

The dim lighting was raised a notch as Jake ordered two bottles of Cabernet and a liter of Absinthe, the elixir of poets and artists. The waiter accepted his gratuity with a smile and left them to their own means of pleasure.

Jake examined the surroundings, noting the exquisite balcony boxes high above the floor, each with a gentleman or two in evening attire and at least two pale skinned women of rare porcelain beauty, laughing politely and bathing their guests with gentle grace.

He noted where the velvet curtains parted, clearing a path for the ventilation system to pull smoke filled air out and pump clean air in.

The stage, where the musicians were busy loading their equipment as technicians prepared for the next act, was large and deep with elaborate theatre lighting and red velvet curtains.

The crowd, seated at tables and along two bars at either side of the hall, was mostly white while the stagehands and help, except for the attending porcelain women, was almost entirely black. The hall was nearly full and hushed with whispered anticipation.

Applause started and grew to an ovation as the master of ceremonies, a striking man familiar to everyone in the underground, a man who went by his title only, emerged from off stage and approached a standing mike.

Jake recognized him at a glance.

"Ladies and gentlemen," announced the Marquis. His initial focus tipped the location of Pale Louie in his balcony perch to Jake's right, close to the stage where three of his favorite porcelain beauties leaned out for a better view.

"We have arrived at that point in the evening you have all anticipated. I present for your pleasure, the wondrous, the exquisite, the incomparably passionate jewel of New Orleans: Ms Ruby Daulton!"

The curtains parted, exposing Ruby in a full blue velvet gown, leaning on a stool with her head bowed and her eyes closed. The crowd swooned and some began to cry before she even raised her head.

Ruby sang.

What has happened down here is the winds have changed
Clouds rolled in from the north and it started to rain
Rained real hard and it rained for a real long time

Six feet of water in the streets of Evangeline

For the first time Jake understood what was about to happen. Ruby had drilled beneath the layers of revelry and good times and jazz and centuries of culture tuned to moss and stone and secret knowledge of spirits and voodoo magic. Ruby, in her altered state, had arrived at the core, at the very heart of New Orleans. She knew without knowing that something very big was coming and her name was Katrina.

Ruby sang.

> *Louisiana, Louisiana*
> *They're trying to wash us away*
> *They're trying to wash us away*

He understood as well that Ruby was not in immediate danger from her captor. She was drugged or stoned and her feet were not planted on solid ground but Pale Louie would not harm her. She was his prize, his treasure, his most precious possession, and he would risk his own life to protect her or to stop anyone who tried to take her from him.

> *The river rose all day*
> *And the river rose all night*
> *Some people got lost in the flood*
> *Some people got away all right*

By the time Ruby finished the song even the waiters were choking back tears, struggling to maintain professional decorum. In New Orleans, decorum must be maintained but they knew too well what was happening. They all knew. The Randy Newman song was written about the hurricane of 1927 but it might have been written in 1912, 1913, 1935, 1947, 1965, 1969 or tomorrow. Everyone knew.

Ruby composed herself, allowing her audience to regain its composure as well. She looked out across the sea of darkness, barely visible faces and fixed for only a moment on Jake. A sorrow was drawn on her expression beyond anything he had seen before. She was reaching through the looking glass, swimming through the liquid green vision of an ancient brew, and trying to recall the face and the place but unable to remember anything beyond the feeling. She mouthed a song title to her piano man and he began to play.

Ruby sang.

It cost me a lot
But there's one thing that I've got
It's my man

Cold or wet
Tired, you bet
All of this I'll soon forget
With my man

Jake pulled himself from a trance that threatened him with paralysis and politely asked a bartender to direct him to a restroom. He walked down a blue velvet corridor and came face to face with a familiar figure.

"We meet again," said the Marquis.

Jake was startled but hardly surprised. He felt no fear. Whatever fears he once harbored, they were buried and transformed by his devotion and determination to his cause. The Marquis opened a curtain, revealing a stone chiseled passage that opened to the underground and led to virtually everywhere in the Quarters, extending outward like tentacles to the outer parishes.

They stepped behind the velvet curtains before the Marquis continued.

"If you think Louie did not notice where Ruby fixed her gaze, you are a bigger fool than I am for helping you."

> *Oh, my man, I love him so*
> *He'll never know*
> *All my life is just a spare*
> *But I don't care*
> *When he takes me in his arms*
> *The world is bright*
> *All right*
>
> *What's the difference if I say*
> *I'll go away*
> *When I know I'll come back*
> *On my knees someday*
>
> *For whatever my man is*
> *I'm his forevermore*

Ruby sang from the depths of her bottomless soul and all of New Orleans welcomed her to its warm and loving eternal embrace.

SCENE 22: MICE AND MEN

FADE IN:

EXTERIOR – KATRINA IN FLORIDA – DAY

Palms bend, cars float, rooftops and debris fly in a hurricane wind. An anonymous voice sings an adaptation of Randy Newman's LOUISIANA 1927.

> *President Bush came down in a big airplane*
> *Met a little white man with a notebook in his hand*
> *President say to the little white man: Aint it a shame*
> *What the storm has done to this poor jungle land*

Ruby's voice takes over, singing.

> *Louisiana, Louisiana*
> *They're trying to wash us away*
> *They're trying to wash us away*

Scenes of destruction continue amidst media updates tracking the storm into the Gulf heading toward New Orleans. Fade slowly to black. We hear the rain like a jackhammer building to a crescendo.

> *Number nine, number nine, number nine…*

....

It was not in Jake's nature to abandon anyone in a crisis and even if it were, he would not abandon his companions now. They were Monk's people and they were in grave danger.

The last time he placed his trust in the Marquis on the Mississippi Queen, he ended up unconscious in a Memphis hotel room. He had little choice back then and he no better options now. This was supposed to be a trial run. His intention was to map the layout, scout security measures and observe their reaction to a staged disruption in the streets. His intention was to use their patterns of behavior and exploit their weaknesses. His intentions died with the realization that Pale Louie had spotted him.

He had no choice but to level with the Marquis and hope for the best. Despite their prior exchange or perhaps because of it, there was something about the Marquis that pulled him into his confidence. Jake did not trust many by raw instinct but he wanted to trust the Marquis. Even though he was drugged and planted in a Memphis hotel, it was not a betrayal of trust; it was business. The Marquis made good on his gambling debt and provided the clues he needed to track Ruby down. He had kept his faith with Pale Louie but he had also assisted Jake when he might have dumped him in a black water grave.

It was more than that. It was how the Marquis regarded Ruby – with as much respect and dignity as circumstances allowed. Like all of New Orleans, like Pale Louie himself, the Marquis was in love. Unlike his master, he did not wish to possess the object of his desire; he wished to win her by his manner and his deeds.

Jake quickly explained the situation and laid out a plan. He would return to the concert and take his seat. It was half past the hour. At precisely 9:45, there would be a series of explosions and a great deal of commotion on Burgandy Street. No one would be hurt but several explosives would be placed in sewer lines so it would register in the concert hall.

They were counting on a rush of security to street level and, in the ensuing commotion and panic, Jake would grab Ruby from the stage while the Marquis escorted his companions to the underground passage. They would count on the Marquis to lead them to the surface.

The Marquis did not like to improvise. He had survived in a chaotic and dangerous world by caution and methodical calculation but there was no time for contingencies. Against his better judgment, he agreed and Jake walked calmly back to his table.

The Marquis re-entered the hall, whispered instructions to his companions, who played it cool, as if it was understood, as if nothing could surprise them in this sorry world of chaos and disorder, a world of indifference to suffering, a world that dished out trouble more often than not, and a world that was going to get real hard real fast. Outside the rain was pounding like the drumbeat of destiny.

As the clock inched forward toward the moment of deliverance, Ruby began singing the same song he had heard on the streets in the lower ninth ward. She was in her own universe, sheltered and protected, but she was somehow connected to the outside world as if by a spiritual umbilical cord. Ruby sang and most everyone in the hall joined in. They were all connected. They were all one.

> *Rain come down like a runaway train*
> *Listen to the pouring rain lord*
> *Listen to the pouring rain*

Ruby saw what they saw, felt what they felt and knew what they knew.

> *Levees gonna break like a shotgun blast*
> *Listen to the pouring rain lord*
> *Listen to the pouring rain*

> *Get out now and get out fast*
> *Listen to the pouring rain*
> *Listen to the pouring rain*

At that moment, as if on cue, an explosion rang out, sounding like it came from within the hall, shattering all sense of order and safety, leaving them a sliver away from total panic and anarchy.

The band stopped playing and Ruby stopped singing, her expression of wonder as if awakening from one dream and entering another where the pieces did not fit.

A large man with a private security badge took the stage and instructed the crowd to remain seated and calm when a volley of explosions, more muted and distant, rang out from above. The man repeated his orders as security personnel ran to hidden stairwells and a first wave of the crowd rushed toward the elevator. Punches thrown, screams, yelling and Jake saw his chance, breaking for the stage as the security chief joined his guards fighting back the mob.

He felt Pale Louie's focus as he grabbed Ruby by the shoulders and stared into her eyes. She did not recognize him. She did not know who he was. She knew he was someone familiar and warm but she could not place him and she was unwilling to follow him.

"Number nine," said Jake. "Number nine."

Ruby remembered knights on white horses, princes in fairy tales and guardian angels. She remembered Kansas and carnivals and then she remembered Jake. She remembered Jake and let go.

He carried her from the stage and dashed down the aisle, down the hallway and behind the curtain to the passage where he was pleased to find the Marquis and his companions waiting. He asked Ruby if she could walk, holding her as she stood. The Marquis produced a vial and instructed her to sniff. It steadied her and cleared her mind enough to answer "yes." She could walk. If need be, she could run.

They began walking as fast as Ruby could manage through a maze of dark tunnels, illuminated by a small flashlight the Marquis garnered from the bar. In the distance behind them, they could hear someone yelling and someone pursuing. They quickened their pace, Ruby and Monk's ladies hiking their skirts and holding their shoes in their hands.

They took a sudden turn and then another until it seemed they were backtracking, running in circles, and Jake became wary. He grabbed the Marquis' shoulder and pulled him close.

"On your honor," demanded Jake. "Is this the way

out?"

The Marquis nodded and Jake believed him. They were circling to lose the hunters who appeared to be closing the distance between them. On a gamble that Louie was not among them, the Marquis led them to a hiding place, a closed space with a false wall concealing its presence, he whispered for them to be silent and they waited until the sound of their pursuers came and went. They waited until they could be sure they were not returning, and then they proceeded in another direction to a stairwell that lifted them from the underground into a back alley in the Quarters.

Monk's women cursed and railed at the stars, the pounding rain and the howling wind. Ruby folded into Jake's arms, painting his face with a lover's kisses. The Marquis politely withdrew, descending once again into the underground where he would attempt to cover his trail.

He would now find out who was a better poker player: himself or Pale Louie.

They called Bones and stayed out of sight until the limousine showed and honked twice. The women took turns telling their stories on the ride back to the safe house on Prieur. Ruby fell asleep on Jake's shoulder while Jake looked into the future.

He was worried: worried that things had not gone as planned, worried that Louie would track them down, worried that Monk and his people were in trouble because of him, and worried that the storm would destroy them all.

The boys were still singing when they reached Prieur Street and several more had joined them with their own rubber boots and yellow slickers. Ruby awakened and smiled as she heard them sing.

Floodwater trap like a ball and chain
Listen to the pouring rain lord
Listen to the pouring rain

It was too late to get out. The roads were closed off.
The trains were not running. Everyone still in New
Orleans was here for the long haul, for better or for
worse.

No one here going to be the same
Katrina was her name lord
Katrina was her name

Ruby was feeling fine. She was safe and secure in
the arms of her lover, her hero, her guardian angel.
Everything was right with the world and dreams really
do come true.

SCENE 23: KATRINA'S WRATH

FADE IN:

EXTERIOR - GREATER NEW ORLEANS - ARIEL
VIEW - NIGHT

Hurricane Katrina approaches New Orleans and the
Gulf coast. ZOOM IN on the lower ninth ward: A
house on North Prieur Street where RUBY rests in
JAKE'S arms on a tattered sofa, an eerie silence and the
illumination of a single lantern.

EXTERIOR - MONTAGE: WAR AND PEACE -
NIGHT AND DAY

The wet, glimmering, silent streets of New Orleans,
subdued drinking in the Quarters, blackouts in the
outer parishes, juxtaposed by scenes from the Iraq War,
the Golden Mosque shattered, Abu Ghraib, Humvees
exploding, wailing mothers, blood, death and
destruction contrasting with presidential addresses and
retired generals pimping the war effort.

We hear Ruby singing a slow, dark version of Cat
Steven's PEACE TRAIN.

I've been crying lately
Thinking about the world as it is
Why must we go on hating?
Why can't we live in bliss?

Fade to the sound of the howling wind and the
pounding rain slowly becoming calm.

....

They say there is a calm before a storm takes the full
measure of her wrath and so it was in the lower ninth
ward on the night Katrina hit. Before the lights went
out, before the television screens went blank, before the
radios went silent and all electronic forms of
communication went dead, the news was good.

At the last moment, Katrina veered north, hitting
sparsely populated land between New Orleans and
Biloxi. One man's good fortune is another's bad but, in
terms of sheer numbers, it was a majestic blessing that
New Orleans would be spared.

On any other night, with rumors of Armageddon, a
city on the edge of panic, and every criminal mind
looking to take advantage, Pale Louie would have
remained in the dry and secure confines of his castle in
the Quarters until the storm passed and order was
restored.

But this was not any other night. Louie's rage
rattled the chandeliers and sparked a fury of activity in
Burgandy House. Ruby was gone, stolen from him
while he watched helplessly from his balcony perch.
His pride, his wonder, his second lease on life, his

jewel, his one true glimpse of perfection was gone and he could not shake the nauseating sense that someone on the inside had to assist this Indian voodoo spirit guide. How did they escape the underground so quickly and so sure?

He had already reviewed the surveillance tapes. It was not difficult to spot Jake Jones and his companions. Despite some effort at disguise – false license plates, wigs, phony moustache – it was not difficult to identify the driver of the Cadillac limousine that deposited him at Burgandy House as a man who often served the interests of the Monk.

Louie's contacts on the streets reported a black Cadillac limousine heading out of the Quarters not long after the explosion shook the underground.

All signs pointed to the lower ninth ward.

With the storm and all that had transpired it would not be possible to track down the Monk tonight. He would be in hiding, as concerned for Katrina and the lawlessness that would surely follow, as he was for Louie.

Revenge would have to wait.

Aside from everything else, the Marquis, his best and most competent servant, had taken it on his own initiative to seek refuge on the Queen. By the time Louie contacted him, he was already heading north to wait out the storm.

He would settle that score later as well.

Louie personally led a small army of loyal soldiers down to the lower ninth. They pounded on doors, knocking them down when necessary, looking for Jake or Ruby or Bones or the Monk or anyone who knew, saw or heard anything about the black Cadillac limousine that carried Ruby away.

The people were already frightened, huddled together in bathrooms, closets, beneath tables and door jams, anywhere they thought would protect them from Katrina's wrath. They knew Pale Louie or they knew of him and when they saw his face, like a vampire in their darkest nightmare, they took it as an omen, a foreshadowing of doom.

They would have told him anything.

"I aint seen nothing, boss," said a woman with three small children, cramped in a hall closet when Louie's men broke in.

A towering black man, whose empathy had long ago abandoned him in Louie's charge, raised the back of his hand and a child spoke up.

"I did," he said. "Down on Prieur Street. We seen 'em driving down on Prieur, a big black limo."

He pointed in the direction of Reynes Street and Louie narrowed his search.

It was long past midnight when Louie and his men in a small fleet of sports utility vehicles arrived at the corner of Reynes and Prieur. The neighborhood was almost entirely dark and silent except for the wind and the pounding rain.

Louie walked to the center of the intersection, looked up and saw him: The shadow of a man pacing on the second story of a house at 927 Prieur. He smiled at how easily he had hunted down his prey.

Revenge would carry a heavy price. Jake Jones would not die quickly. He would know the kind of pain no man should ever know, even in his darkest nightmares, until he told everything he could tell. Then he would suffer more.

Louie rationalized that it was only good business. Those who crossed him, defied his wishes, insulted or betrayed him would know that the consequences were merciless and severe. The truth was: Louie was a sadistic monster who enjoyed the face, the sounds and the vision of pain.

He savored the moment, anticipating, visualizing what was about to happen, raising his hand and instructing his men to close ranks behind him.

Jake opened the curtain above and felt a river of terror wash over him.

Louie smiled as their eyes met for the first time.

Something was happening. A sound like a ship ripped from its bearings broke through the howling wind and the rain. Louie's men looked around in horror. The high pitched, screaming sound of metal beams twisting and bending rose and the ground beneath the street, beneath the houses and buildings began to quake.

Jake saw the terror that only moments ago entered his soul, rendering him helpless, filling him with paralyzing fear, transferred to the soul of Pale Louie.

He could not move as a blast shattered the quiet, unsuspecting neighborhood. It was the sound of the levee breaking replaced in an instant with the sound of a river swallowing the streets of the lower ninth.

Louie and all his men were swept away like rats in sewer water. The floodwaters of the Industrial Canal would batter them against concrete, brick walls, road signs, houses, cars and uprooted trees, until it found its crest and backtracked, carrying Louie in the undercurrent back down the canal, depositing his lifeless corpse in the waters of Lake Pontchartrain where a thousand souls, victims of Louie's life of revenge, waited to welcome him home.

Ruby awakened in horror and rushed to Jake's side, clinging to him for strength and courage as they watched the floodwaters roll in like a thundering train, rising until it seemed no one would get out alive.

When the rising waters stopped short of sweeping them away, when it seemed the house would hold on to its foundation, when the shaking and roar subsided, Ruby cried and Jake held her firm. Ruby cried for New Orleans and all the people who were not as lucky as they were and would not survive the night. Ruby cried for a world and a god and a lifetime that could create such an endless chain of nightmares and suffering.

Ruby cried and every citizen of New Orleans went into a mourning that would not abate for years.

Someday, not so far into the future, when the wounds of that night were beginning to heal, the boys of Prieur Street would hear the story and sing:

Pale Louie dead and gone
Didn't leave no one to moan

Pale Louie dead and gone
Didn't leave no one to mourn

Look out yonder where the levee gave way
Pale Louie dead and gone

You can see Pale Louie floating away
Pale Louie dead and gone

Look out yonder where the levee gave way
Pale Louie dead and gone

You can see Pale Louie in a watery grave
Pale Louie dead and gone

Pale Louie dead and gone
Didn't leave no one to pray

Pale Louie dead and gone
There aint much more to say

SCENE 24: WAR ZONE

FADE IN:

EXTERIOR -- NEW ORLEANS – DAY

We see scenes of mass destruction, disorder and chaos
in the aftermath of Hurricane Katrina: Bodies floating,
women crying, dogs running, looting and violence,
children pleading for help, cars overturned, trees
uprooted, homes destroyed, on and on.

INTERIOR – AIR FORCE ONE – DAY

We see the president looking out the window of Air
Force 1, surveying the damage below. Cut to the
president with FEMA Director Michael Brown. The
president says, "You're doing a heck of a job, Brownie."

EXTERIOR – SUPERDOME – DAY

The people, ushered to the Superdome, are pleading for
water and food. A CNN reporter looks into the
camera, shaking his head: "Where is the National
Guard?" Footage of Katrina destruction continues as
we hear John Fogerty's FORTUNATE SON.

Some folks are born made to wave the flag
Ooh, they're red white and blue
And when the band plays hail to the chief
Ooh, they point the cannon at you, lord

It aint me, it aint me,
I aint no senator's son, son
It aint me, it aint me,
I aint no fortunate one, no

Fade song. Fade scene to black.

....

The politicians kept warning the people that the war would follow us home someday. Looking out over the destruction in morning light, Jake wondered if it already had.

It was a war zone. The decimation was so complete it was a miracle any man, woman or child in the lower ninth had survived. It was a miracle their house was left standing. All around them, block after block, from the Claiborne Bridge to Florida Avenue and beyond, homes were reduced to rubble, cars overturned in fallen trees, bodies floating face down in waters mixed with a toxic brew of sewage, gas and chemicals. Power lines were down and barges from the Industrial Canal deposited where homes used to be.

Ruby stood by Jake's side, holding tight to choke back her tears. She had already spent them all in a night of horrors, when the only sounds were people crying, dogs yelping and isolated gunshots against a wall of thick, watery silence. Nobody slept.

They spent most of the morning sitting on the upstairs balcony, absorbing the breadth of destruction, watching planes and helicopters survey the damage and survivors making their way to nearby Claiborne Bridge. They were too near the levee break for casual visitors, the putrid water settling at six or more feet and brewing in the lilting sun. There were no rescue efforts here, not in the lower ninth where the people were mostly black and poor.

Here in the lower ninth, they were safe from looters and criminal gangs. Of the seven parishes of Greater New Orleans, St. Bernard was low on the list of treasures to be looted and the lower ninth was in a class by itself.

By noon, the liquid heat was debilitating and they knew they had to get out. If they remained where they were, they would die of hunger, thirst or disease. They would die because no one thought or cared to rescue them.

With only cursory knowledge of the terrain, they were mapping out a plan with pencil on paper when Bones floated up on a yellow life raft with another in tow. He looked a hundred years older but he wore a smile of deep relief that Jake and Ruby were still alive.

He threw a rope ladder up and climbed it rather than wade through the toxic mix. He offered bottles of drinking water before he sat down with an expression of doom.

"Well, I've got good news and bad but I won't lie, it's mostly bad."

"What could be worse than this," said Ruby with a gesture to the desolation surrounding them, stretching as far as they could see.

Bones gazed at her with genuine admiration. Like most of the jazz legends that made their mark in the Big Easy, she was even more impressive up close and in the flesh.

"Looking at you and Jake here," he replied, " I am reminded it could be a lot worse. We all heard what happened with Pale Louie and we're all hoping its true."

Jake assured him Louie was as dead as a fly wrapped in a widow's web.

"That's the good news," said Bones. "Here's the bad."

He gave them the lowdown, straight and sober. Most of New Orleans, all of St. Bernard and Orleans parishes, was under water. Monk had survived but a lot of his people were dead. His mama was sick and hurt. His grandma was old, weak and needed her medicine.

"Monk got to get down there," said Bones.

Jake and Ruby understood. They were on their own.

They all felt bad there wasn't more they could do but in New Orleans blood family came first. Bones himself had family scattered in the flood zones and figured he would spend the better part of a week tracking them down and seeing to their needs.

The word on the street said the police were no different than anyone else: They abandoned their duty to take care of their own. The police were only a sliver better than street thugs anyways. It was anarchy. It was everyman and everywoman for themselves.

"Monk says if you live through it, he'll do all he can to help you rebuild. He sent you these here things."

He pulled up a large bundle with bottled water, a change of clothes and walking shoes for Ruby, a good flashlight, a canister of butane, canned food, a Swiss army knife and a battery powered pump for the raft.

"You're going to need these here things," he explained. "Whatever you do, you don't want to stay here. If you aint dead already when the water dries up, they just as soon bulldoze your house with you in it. You want to live and you damn well better, you got to get out of the lower ninth. They don't call this Arabi for nothing."

Jake and Ruby did not ask what he meant. They knew. Anyone in the lower ninth was presumed a criminal low life just like anyone Arab was presumed a terrorist. Time was too short to fully appreciate the ironies but they were as rich as an insurance executive's bank account.

"Most of the people is heading for the Superdome or the Convention Center."

Bones stretched out a map and laid out a route down Claiborne to Interstate 10, explaining that the interstate was high enough to be dry but everything else except the bridge over the Industrial Canal was flooded. They could walk down the interstate to the Superdome.

"I don't know." He shook his head. "Heard some bad things but I don't know any other alternatives. Soon as I round up my own, we'll be heading out the same way."

Ruby suggested that they team up and go together but Bones was still shaking his head only more so.

"Family aint like me," he said. "They don't trust no strangers and they aint about to travel with a white woman as pretty as you. Don't matter who you are.

"One more thing," he said quietly. "You got a gun?"

Jake pulled Ruby's small caliber pistol out of his pocket.

"That's nice," said Bones as he unwrapped a .350 magnum with a box of bullets.

"Take it," he demanded. "You're going to need it. You don't know what New Orleans is like when the lights go down. Don't trust nobody. Not the police, not the rescue workers, not the army, no one.

"Monk says hide your money – if you got any left – but take it with you. Don't let nobody be searching you and if you got to show your gun, be ready to use it."

It was a hard lesson but it had to be said and there was no time to put it in gentle terms. If they wanted to live, they would have to get hard fast. What else was new? Their whole lives seemed a preparation for the next trial, the next crisis or the next tragedy.

They shared a moment of clarity, looking out at the devastation and Bones choked up, his eyes welling with tears. Ruby embraced him, steadied him and held him to the solid ground of his people. They all understood. It was time to be strong for all the people who could not be strong, for all the ones that would break under the strain. It was time for the strong to stand.

Bones must have apologized a dozen times before he was satisfied they understood and would do the same. He left with the smile that set him apart from most everyone else, feeling a lot better than when he came.

Ruby had the shakes of withdrawal from the drugs

Pale Louie fed her but she would do her share. She could always count on an inner strength when she needed it and it seemed she needed it often.

It was near dusk when they were packed and ready to roll: a crescent moon over the crescent city and a mix of swarming insects with the still sweltering heat was almost unbearable yet it would only get worse.

They floated over to the Claiborne Bridge. The currents of the canal were much too strong to ford so they dragged the raft over the bridge and resumed paddling east through the streets of St. Bernard, stopping to talk and exchange stories along the way.

They refused to take on passengers. It was hard but the people who asked, always for someone else, an elderly woman or a child, always understood. It was the danger of rescuing a drowning man. It was the uncertainty of where they were headed and whether it would be any better than where they were. If a child or an old woman is going to die anyway, it was better they should die in the arms of someone they knew and loved. The people knew but they had to ask and Jake and Ruby had to refuse with a promise to send help if they could.

It was late and they were dragging like miners at the end of a shift when they finally reached the interstate. Even in the dim light of a last quarter moon, what they had seen filled their hearts with sorrow. They traded the raft for a shopping cart and made camp with hundreds, maybe thousands of others, on the high, dry concrete ground over New Orleans.

Huddled together, Ruby's shakes ebbing and flowing without a word of complaint, they heard explosions and saw black clouds rising over the dark city. The only signs of active life, besides the can fires of the abandoned masses, came from the south where the French Quarters and the Garden District were illuminated like beacons of hope.

Here on the overpass and throughout the rest of New Orleans, isolated bursts of gunfire and darkness reigned. Fear and helplessness were palpable. The heartbeat of the city of jazz was muted and dim. They took turns pretending to sleep, all the while reflecting, absorbing, comprehending and knowing:

This was what it was like to live with war.

Number nine, number nine, number nine...

SCENE 25: THE BRIDGE TO FREEDOM

FADE IN:

EXTERIOR – DISASTER-WAR MONTAGE – NIGHT
AND DAY

As before, we see scenes of devastation from the wars
in Iraq and Afghanistan juxtaposed with scenes of
desperation in New Orleans after Katrina. We hear the
voice of Neil Young from the album LIVING WITH
WAR.

> *I'm living with war in my heart*
> *I'm living with war in my heart in my mind*
> *I'm living with war right now*
>
> *Don't take no tidal wave*
> *Don't take no mass grave*
> *Don't take no smoking gun*
> *To show how the west was won*
> *But when the curtain falls, I pray for peace*
> *Try to remember peace*

The song fades, replaced by John Lennon's YER BLUES
from the White Album.

EXTERIOR – INTERSTATE 10 – ARIEL VIEW – DAY

We see the abandoned multitudes of Katrina victims walking toward the Superdome. ZOOM IN to Jake and Ruby among them.

> *Yes, I'm lonely wanna die*
> *Yes, I'm lonely wanna die*
> *If I aint dead already*
> *Girl you know the reason why*
>
> *The eagle picks my eye*
> *The worm he licks my bone*
> *I feel so suicidal*
> *Just like Dylan's Mr. Jones*

EXTERIOR – SUPERDOME – DAY

The swarming mass of dirty, hungry, thirsty and desperate people, standing outside the Superdome, plead desperately for help.

Fade to black.

....

Jake and Ruby walked with the multitudes, like a giant serpent, in one direction, one mind, one heart, one soul, toward the Superdome, towering in the distance like a desperate prayer.

Along the previous day's journey and during the night, they heard stories, each grimmer than the last, about what was going down inside the colossal dome.

In the back of his mind, Jake knew it was a false

prayer, a prayer to a false god or rather to men in power that did not carry the interests of the people in their hearts. One look at Ruby and he knew she was thinking the same thing: They had to find another way.

They had to get away from the mindless throng being herded like cattle to an enclosed space where they could be watched and controlled. It was like the Cherokee, rounded up and herded into cattle yards before the long walk on the trail of tears to the unwanted lands of Oklahoma. The scattered police and guards were not there to protect them or show them the way; they were there to keep them from escaping.

The last thing the authorities wanted was a mass infusion of desperately poor, homeless, sick and dying people into the French Quarters, where adventuresome tourists celebrated Katrina's wrath, or the Garden District where the privileged remained relatively dry and well.

When they came to where the people were being ushered off the highway, Jake and Ruby kept going, heads down and hands locked. A guard in plain clothes ordered them to stop. Ruby offered an excuse that they had relatives in Audubon and when Jake slipped him a hundred dollar bill, he let them pass. Without money they would have joined the suffering masses under the dome of endless sorrow.

They headed south by southeast along the expressway, the liquid heat pounding them down with every step until they had to stop, get off the concrete furnace, rest, drink and eat from their diminishing supplies.

Leaving the expressway, they traveled west into the lush, green grounds of the Garden District where private security guards constantly questioned them and warned them to keep walking.

Others who had somehow managed to evade the blockades themselves joined them along the way. They were told that the only way out of New Orleans, where they could cross the Mississippi to relative safety on the West Bank outside the disaster zone, was the Crescent City Bridge to the sister city of Gretna, a majority white working class community that was spared the wrath of the storm. Word was the Gretna authorities were increasingly concerned. It seemed the escape route would not be open long so they should take it while they still could.

The light of day was fading but the relentless humidity was not and their bodies were stiff and trembling. They chose a moment when no one seemed to be watching, ducking into a garden where they slept like exhausted children through the lonely night.

In the morning, they ate a can of cold soup and discovered that they were no more than half a mile from their new destination: the bridge to freedom.

Jake still had plenty enough money to buy transport if only they could get out of New Orleans. They could take refuge for a week or two, count their blessings and make a plan for the rest of their lives.

After all this time and all they had been through, they had nearly forgotten that Ruby was no longer a wanted woman. She was free of the mob, free of Pale Louie and as free of her past as it was possible to be. She had a career as a singer and a universe of possibilities were opening to her like a rose in magnificent bloom. Ruby had a home, a circle of loved ones and roots that ran deeper than she could ever have dreamed.

As they approached the bridge, they found dozens of people with the same idea, all relieved to have come this far, convinced that the nightmare would end on the other side of the river, all wearing smiles of weary satisfaction.

Half way across, their smiles were wiped away. A mob of armed, grim-faced men, all white, some uniformed, many more in civilian clothes, stopped them in their tracks with rifles and shotguns poised for action.

What happened next no one would ever decipher. A shot rang out and a volley of gunfire followed. The people panicked and ran. Jake stepped in front of Ruby, taking a bullet in the chest. The law and order mob on the Gretna side of the bridge moved forward and the rabble on the New Orleans side retreated, leaving Jake bleeding on the pavement and Ruby hovering over him, crying, cursing and comforting.

A man Ruby had never seen before, a short but broad shouldered black man with the huge, strong hands of a workingman, kneeled beside her.

"I don't know who this man is but I do know one thing," he said. "He put his life on the line so you could live."

Her mind truly clear for the first time in days, maybe weeks (she could not tell), tears streaming from her eyes, falling on the wound of her fallen lover, her savior, her guardian protector, she looked at the angry mob fronted by officers of the law, marching forward, she looked back at the retreating, beleaguered citizens of an abandoned city, she gazed into Jake's eyes, life still clinging to his broken body, and found the strength that enabled her to survive a thousand crises, a thousand assaults on her dignity, an endless chain of attempts to break her spirit and she refused to give in.

"I can't leave him," she said. "I won't."

The man knew by raw instinct there was no point in arguing. At a time like this, after all they had suffered, common sense made no sense at all.

"Can you walk?" he asked.

"Hell, yes!" she replied.

"Then help me stand him up. We got to get off this bridge!"

He hoisted Jake over his shoulder and they began to walk at a measured pace back to the city of misery, disease and death, where even dogs were shot down in the streets for having the audacity to survive and roam freely, where human beings fared little better, abandoned on rooftops, left for dead, wandering the streets through toxic waters, abandoned in the crushing heat of hospitals and old folks homes, abandoned in the city of jazz to form once again an ancient bond to the music that defined them: gospel and the blues.

Bullets still flying overhead but no longer aimed at human flesh, the message received loud and clear: no visitors allowed, no lost souls, no black trash, no abandoned, needy people, they made their way to a sheltered refuge away from the docks, away from the madness, where Ruby struggled to keep Jake conscious.

The man went out to beg, hustle and steal what he thought they needed and came back with a roll of gauze, duct tape, iodine, a bottle of whiskey and a pair of needle-nose pliers. They started a fire, grateful that it was still daylight so it would not attract attention, and heated the pliers.

"Hold him," the man said as he placed a stick in Jake's mouth and plied him with whiskey.

Jake's body lifted off the ground, taut and trembling, as the man pulled the bullet out. They used Jake's knife, heated in fire, to seal the wound, bound him with gauze and tape, and treated his fever with cold rags through the remains of the day.

As the sun was setting on yet another terrifying day in New Orleans, where so much of the outer parishes were under siege, where the poor were allowed to live and buy homes under a cloud of inevitable doom, this man with tear-stained eyes, a man who might have lost everything he had and loved, apologized for having to leave them.

"I got to take care of my own," he cried.

Ruby hugged him, kissed and thanked him from the depths of her soul. She promised him they would be all right. She promised him they would survive.

"What's your name?" she called out as he walked back into the endless nightmare.

"They call me Bubba," he replied. "If we live through this, I'll look you up."

It was the first real glimmer of hope she had heard or seen since the ordeal of Katrina began and it warmed her heart.

She had bottled water, candles and everything she could think of to treat Jake's wound. There was little more to do but hunt down food and wait by his side.

Ruby prayed to every deity she could think of or imagine. She prayed for the city, for the poor and disabled, for the nation that allowed it to happen, and for Jake – mostly for Jake.

Fifteen hundred miles away, a wise old man

awakened from an afternoon nap and sent his spirit to look after his favorite son. In the spirit world, where Jake now resided, he heard his mentor's chant and Ruby's prayers and he was not afraid. He was worried and consumed with sorrow but he was not afraid.

It was as if all of New Orleans had been transported back in time to a long lost era – before technology, before industry, before electricity and indoor plumbing. With each day and every sweltering night, more bodies would be seen floating face down in the water-filled streets, more would be sick and dying from the putrid water, more would be trapped, gunned down or terrorized and the further they would move back in time.

Most would refuse to give up the civilized nature of their beings. Most would refuse to yield to the law of the jungle, survival of the strongest, kill or be killed, but few could not understand and feel sympathy for those who fell short.

Beneath the misery and misfortune, there was a brooding rage. There was a promise broken. There was a bloodline and a vow of belonging to the greatest nation on earth, torn and shattered.

Number nine, number nine, number nine…

SCENE 26: THE HEALING

FADE IN:

EXTERIOR – NEW ORLEANS – UNDER A FREEWAY
OVERPASS – NIGHT

We hear the boys from the lower ninth ward circled
around a fire in a barrel singing.

>*Whole world tumbling like a rolling stone*
>*Got to be peace someday, lord*
>*Got to be peace someday*
>*Every man for himself, every woman alone*
>*Got to be peace someday, lord*
>*Got to be peace someday*
>
>*Whole world is crying*
>*Too many people are dying*

EXTERIOR – NEW ORLEANS – DISASTER
MONTAGE – NIGHT AND DAY

Recovery efforts, helicopter rescues, and floating search
and rescue teams interspersed with scenes of looting,
crime, police abuse and general devastation. The boys
of Prieur Street are singing:

Our leaders promise to deliver hope
Got to be peace someday, lord
But all they give us is a little rope
Got to be peace someday

Oh lord, won't you hear my prayer
Whole world is crying
Don't want a free ride, just a modest fare
Too many people are dying

Got to be peace someday, lord
Got to be peace someday

. . . .

Like most everything else in New Orleans, hospitals were not functioning. Ruby had to keep Jake alive the best she could until help arrived. On the third day, when his skin went cold and she thought she would lose him, she met someone from the lower ninth who promised to deliver a message to the Monk that they desperately needed help.

Ruby prayed and Jake held on. In desperation she stood on the street and sang and people recognized her voice. They gathered around her, gave her clean water, food, medicine, whiskey, advice – anything she thought Jake needed, anything that would ease the pain.

On the fourth day, a doctor from the lower ninth came calling. Unlike government officials, politicians or federal agencies, Monk was a man of his word. A couple of his men put Jake on a stretcher and carried him to a riverfront warehouse that was being converted to a makeshift clinic. Jake was its first patient.

"If he aint dead yet," the doctor assured Ruby, "he aint going to die."

Ruby stayed by his side until he could stand, until he could walk, and until he could be moved safely to a home in Gentilly. No one would be returning to the ninth ward for a very long time but the Monk was a man of his word.

Jake's wound healed. The wounds of Katrina would not. Every man, woman and child who witnessed the tragic chain of events, took a solemn vow never to forget. The more they learned, the greater their discontent.

People died, lost their homes, their livelihoods and the city that nurtured and defined them as much from government indifference and neglect as from a natural disaster. Shoddy engineering, substandard materials, negligent maintenance and politics as usual (poor people do not vote) led to levee failures and mass flooding that Katrina herself should not have caused. Rumors persisted that the levees were blown to relieve pressure and save the rich neighborhoods. The rumors may have been false but the sentiment that breathed life into them was not.

When they learned that a hurricane hitting New Orleans was among the highest ranking potential disasters in the nation yet little or nothing was done to prepare for it, while billions went to a war that should never have been fought, the people knew the war had come home.

The war had come home and the poor people of the lower ninth, Jefferson and Orleans parishes were scattered with the four winds. For those lucky enough to land a substandard, asbestos infested, cancer causing emergency trailer on a concrete lot outside Baton Rouge, Houston or Salt Lake City, New Orleans would become a tortured memory and an open wound.

The city of jazz would never be the same.

For Jake, New Orleans was always foreign terrain. He respected the city by instinct and adapted to her by necessity but only in time would she invade his desert soul and capture his heart. In time, he understood that the people of New Orleans were his brothers and sisters. Like the indigenous tribes of all nations, the land belonged to the people who lived, worked, cherished, suffered and died on it far more than their conquerors would ever comprehend.

The common, everyday people were the fruits of the land and their seeds had taken root. Their souls, their culture and ancestry, were intimately entwined with the land itself. New Orleans could not exist without them and they could not exist without New Orleans.

In time he came to love them as he did his blood family and they welcomed him as one of their own. In time he would come to know New Orleans as his home and though he would always feel the pull of the land that shaped and nurtured *his* soul, he would carry her with him wherever he went and she would never leave his thoughts or affection.

When he was well enough, Jake lent his hand in rebuilding New Orleans from the ground up, repairing her broken bones, closing her wounds, easing her mind, soothing her soul, and as she regained her strength, he regained his and Ruby regained her own.

She was legendary before Katrina; after Katrina, her legend soared like a bald eagle on the crosswinds in Grand Canyon. She turned down offers from record executives and high-powered Madison Avenue agents. She gave her career to the man who saved her man. Monk was a man of his word.

She refused money gigs at casinos and tourist traps, preferring a little underground jazz joint just outside the Quarters. If people wanted to see and hear Ruby Daulton, they had to find their way; they had to visit the real New Orleans. They had to be guided by a local in the know. They had to inquire with a cabbie who would look them over, sound them out and either show them the way or tell them she was a ghost, a legend who did not really exist.

Some said she channeled the soul of Lady Day but, like Billie and Bessie and Ella and Etta, she had a style that belonged only to her. Her versions of Don't Explain, My Man, Blind Girl, St. Louis Blues, Backwater Blues and so many others carried a quiet, lilting quality that soothed and comforted the beaten, downtrodden and dispossessed souls of survivors. Her rendition of Strange Fruit, the song that reputedly accompanied far too many suicides, somehow gave comfort to the suffering masses.

Southern trees bear strange fruit
Blood on the leaves and blood at the root
Black bodies swinging in the southern breeze
Strange fruit hanging from the poplar trees

Ruby sang the blues and New Orleans gradually, slowly healed.

On quiet nights, with the ghosts of Katrina still hovering in the liquid darkness, all of New Orleans turned out the lights and listened with their collective heart. Jake took his seat at a corner table, joining Bones, Monk, the Marquis and sometimes a broad-shouldered black man who went by the name of Bubba, and cried for a city still struggling to survive.

The city cried with him.

There were tears of sorrow for all the hardships that had befallen them, tears of mourning for those who were lost, and tears of joy in knowing they had survived to lead the country in the great healing.

The people would not allow New Orleans to die. No matter how long it took, no matter what obstacles were thrown in their path, they would rebuild. If it took a hundred years they would rebuild.

Ruby was New Orleans and she could not be defeated by a dozen hurricanes or a thousand years of misfortune. After all that had happened, she was still standing, defiant and strong. She survived to thrive and prosper and Jake was by her side.

Them that's got shall get
Them that's not shall lose
So the Bible said and it still is news
Mama may have, papa may have
But God bless the child that's got his own

Ruby sang and the seeds of hope, the seeds of courage and endurance, were planted in the fertile ground of the people of New Orleans.

SCENE 27: NUMBER NINE

FADE IN:

INTERIOR – MONK'S PLACE – NIGHT

Ruby shines in a spotlight on stage. She sings Bonnie Raitt's ballad I CAN'T MAKE YOU LOVE ME.

> *Turn down the lights*
> *Turn down the bed*
> *Turn down these voices inside my head*
> *Lay down with me*
> *Tell me no lies*
> *Just hold me close, don't patronize*
> *Don't patronize me*
>
> *'Cause I can't make you love me if you don't*
> *You can't make your heart feel something it won't*
> *Here in the dark, in these final hours*
> *I will lay down my heart and I'll feel the power*
> *But you won't, no you won't*
> *'Cause I can't make you love me, if you don't*
>
> *I'll close my eyes, then I won't see*
> *The love you don't feel when you're holding me*
> *Morning will come and I'll do what's right*

Just give me till then to give up this fight
And I will give up this fight

CLOSE UP of the Marquis at a corner table, his face a portrait in sorrow.

The song fades and the screen goes black. We hear the voice of John Lennon.

Number nine, number nine, number nine…

....

   The Marquis was a gentleman's gentleman. Like the Monk, he felt a solemn obligation to protect both Jake and Ruby but especially Ruby. In the wake of Pale Louie's demise, he inherited the throne of the underground kingdom known as the House of Burgandy. In that role, he sent a message to Guido Lazerri in Las Vegas, informing him that recent events had rendered all previous understandings and contracts regarding Ruby Daulton null and void.
   Ruby was at last a free woman, free to remain in New Orleans if she wished and free to go anywhere she wanted to go on this earth. If she desired, the Marquis would personally escort her to every hotel and gambling hall on the Vegas strip. If anyone from Lazerri's crowd offered so much as an unkind word or a derisive glance, the New Orleans underground would raise an army to invade Vegas and the war would leave no one standing.
   Guido wired back that he no longer had any interest in Ruby Daulton except as a singer. If she came to the

strip, he assured the Marquis, she would be paid top dollar, lodged in the finest hotel and treated as a queen.

On a quiet night in Monk's Place, when Ruby finished her last song, the Marquis revealed his given name and a great deal about the person he was and how he came to be.

His name was Anthony La Roche (la row shay). He was a bayou boy who spent his youth known as Tony the Roach, getting into trouble with drugs and petty crime. On one of his forays into the Easy, he was walking through St. Louis Cemetery around dusk when he happened across four thugs accosting a pale-skinned man in a black cape.

On any other night, he might have been one of them but on this night, he identified with the victim. His uncle, a kind and gentle soul, had been mugged only a few nights before and Tony was in the process of re-examining his life. He wore a chain around his waist and carried a crowbar for his own protection. Without a moment's hesitation, he waded into the fight with the strength of blood vengeance, knocking two of the thugs unconscious and sending the others running for cover. In the rush of adrenalin, he did not notice he had taken a knife wound to the gut.

Pale Louie took him in, cared for him, provided an education, trained him in business and the darker arts, and when the time came, he made an offer: He would hold the title of Marquis and become heir to the House of Burgandy. He would become Louie's son in every way but blood. In exchange, he asked only one thing: he had to promise never to see his family again.

From that time forward, Tony the Roach became the Marquis and his family would never know what happened to their boy. Years later, he tried to track them down without success. He heard stories. Some said they left in the middle of the night without a word to anyone. Others said Louie had "taken care of them." He would always wonder if Louie had indeed sealed their fate in a wetland grave.

The Marquis was deeply in love with Ruby but he never said so. Everyone in the underground knew the truth of his devotion, including Jake and Ruby herself.

Jake was not the type of man to waste his time on jealousy. The love he shared with Ruby sprang from the deepest well of affection and trust. It was not possessive. If Ruby wanted to pursue another relationship she was free to do so. They both were but neither had any desire to walk down that path.

Together, against all odds, they had found and made a good life, a fulfilling and contented life. Ruby had at long last found the place she had always belonged, a home for her restless soul. For Jake it was more complicated.

Every year, he made pilgrimage back to Third Mesa and every year he stayed a little longer. The pull of the desert was strong and tied to his soul just as Ruby's was tied to New Orleans. Though there was no disaster to attract the attention of media and politicians, his people were also suffering. Their catastrophe was a daily grind of poverty, homelessness, alcohol, drugs and a new disease born of their culture as warriors in the age of terror: their young were going to war and returning with dark hearts and broken spirits.

He was a man torn between two paths, two families, two tribes and two hearts and he shared his conflicted sentiments with Ruby. They shed tears of sorrow and loss mixed with an understanding that comes when two souls have shared a life in all its richness. They had known the greatest glories and the most profound grief. They had survived the darkest hours and climbed the tallest peaks. They had laughed, cried, fought, mourned and discovered in each other the meaning of existence. They knew love. They knew a love that would never fail, that would always answer the call, a love that would bind their souls and their destinies together forever.

He worked at odd jobs in construction, pounding a hammer, sawing boards, pouring cement, reworking power systems, clearing debris, whatever was needed to rebuild the schools, homes, hospitals and businesses. He volunteered to work on clean-up crews. He worked with movie stars and celebrities, most of whom never showed up but lent their names to the effort.

He worked with lawyers and investigators trying to decipher what happened during those tragic days and nights, when the law turned against the people and justice was abandoned. He did what he could though it was never enough.

He worked hard, long hours and he never complained. At the end of the day, no matter how exhausted he might be, he always went down to Monk's Place and listened to Ruby sing. He sat at a corner table reserved for the Monk and his special guests. On most evenings he would join Monk, the Marquis and Bones for a few drinks to close out the final set.

All and all, it was a good life, hard but good. He helped to rebuild the city by day, listened to his lover at night and held her in his arms until the morning light.

What more could he expect? What more could life have to offer?

Nine years after they arrived in New Orleans, nine years after Katrina and nine years after the levees gave way, he felt the pull of Third Mesa more powerfully than ever. Nine months later he knew he had to go. For a long time he resisted, knowing that once he made the journey this time he might not return. His heart was torn between the land he loved and the woman he loved. The pull of the desert would not loosen its hold.

He told himself the city needed him but he knew in his soul the Rez needed whatever help he could give every bit as much as New Orleans did.

He told himself Ruby needed him but he knew she would survive and thrive without him. She was stronger now than ever, stronger than anyone he knew, and she had people who cared deeply for her and would protect her with their lives.

He knew he could not have both. Ruby belonged in the Easy. It was her home. She could not leave it behind without living the rest of her days in mourning. He would never ask her to do so.

The last few times he called, he sensed that White Wolf was not well. The last time he even said so. For White Wolf to admit illness it had to be gravely serious. Fear took hold in Jake's gut and grew like a seed of anger. He had to go. White Wolf, the man who had been a father to him, who raised and nurtured him as if he was his own blood, was dying.

"Hey, sugar," said Ruby with a smile that would light a cavern in hell. She had just finished her set with *My Man* as she so often did and strolled over to where

Jake sat waiting. They kissed and she knew at once something was wrong.

"What is it?" she implored.

"Sit down, Ruby, we have to talk."

Through all the days she had known him, after all the dangers they had survived, she had never known her silent hero to utter those words. She felt her knees go soft as she sat at the table and asked for a drink to soften the blow. Jake poured her a brandy and waited for her to drink.

"White Wolf is sick," he said. "I believe he's dying."

Tears sprang from Ruby's eyes and rolled down her cheeks. She wiped them away and could not help but smile.

"I'm sorry," she said. "I know he's like a father to you. I don't mean... It's just that I thought you were leaving me."

Jake took her in his arms and everything changed. He knew then he could never leave her. Whatever happened, he would stand by her. Destiny had taken its turn.

Together they left for Third Mesa in Ruby's newly restored 1967 baby blue Dodge Coronet convertible. It felt good to be back on the road, hair flying in the wind, sun shining down on a beautiful summer day.

The shadow of White Wolf lowered upon them as they crossed the Mississippi into Indian Territory and even more so as they left Oklahoma behind. They were flooded with memories of their cross-country journey: Ruby's grandmother in her last days on earth, betrayal in St. Louis, Kachina magic in an Arizona bar, a fateful cruise down the great muddy river and a royal flush in hearts. They had confronted more cruel twists of fate than most people will encounter in a lifetime and emerged stronger, prouder and more defiant than ever.

Tall Woman saw them approaching, a puff of dust in the distance, long before they drove up to the trailer where White Wolf lay dying. She emerged from the shade of the canopy and took them each in her powerful arms.

"He's been waiting for you," she said as she led them to her husband's side.

"How long has it been?" said the old man with a crooked grin. "It seems like yesterday."

"It was yesterday," replied Jake.

He narrowed his eyes at Ruby.

"I see you brought me a gift."

The four of them shared a laugh. The wily old coyote of a man had not changed, not even with death shrouding his spirit.

They spent nine days and nine nights at White Wolf's side. In the evenings they carried him outside so he could watch the moon and admire the desert nightlife. The old man embraced Ruby as the woman who made his son whole and Ruby embraced White Wolf as the father she never had.

In his dying hour he cried for all the suffering people he would no longer be able to help. He asked Jake and Ruby to care for their people as best they could. He told them they need not worry about Tall Woman. She had made arrangements to move in with her sister. He asked them to be true to themselves, true to each other and true to their destinies.

They nodded in solemnity and let the gentle wind, the stars and the spirit of the desert speak for them. White Wolf understood. He howled from the depths of his soul and listened as a lone wolf answered. Coyotes yapped and an owl fluttered overhead. His lips curled into a knowing smile and then, he let go, eyes wide open, a picture of the spirit world still fresh in his vision, his face a reflection of deep satisfaction.

They remained in the desert for nine more days, helping with whatever needed to be done and participating in the rituals of death. They then took the long road back to New Orleans where they would begin the next phase of their lives. They would keep their promise to White Wolf. They would return to Third Mesa every nine months to check on Tall Woman and attend to the needs of the people. They would remain true to themselves, true to each other, and true to their destinies.

FADE IN:

INTERIOR – MONK'S PLACE – NIGHT

We see Ruby on stage and Jake seated at a corner table. Ruby sings BLACKBIRD from the White Album.

> *Blackbird singing in the dead of night*
> *Take these broken wings and learn to fly*
> *All your life*
> *You were only waiting for this moment to arrive*

Fade BLACKBIRD. We hear:

Number nine, number nine, number nine…

Fade REVOLUTION 9 under as The Beatles' HERE COMES THE SUN is heard in the foreground with scenes of a beautiful Gulf sunrise.

Little darling, it's been a long cold lonely winter
Little darling, it feels like years since it's been here
Here comes the sun, here comes the sun
And I say it's all right

Little darling, the smiles returning to the faces
Little darling, it seems like years since it's been here
Here comes the sun, here comes the sun
And I say it's all right

Sun, sun, sun, here it comes
Sun, sun, sun, here it comes
Sun, sun, sun, here it comes

Fade to black. We hear:

Number nine, number nine, number nine…

ABOUT THE AUTHOR

Jack Random has lived both an ordinary and extraordinary life. His roots firmly planted in the fertile central valley of California, he has marched the streets in protest, haunted jazz town bars, read poetry in cafes and town squares, strutted his hour upon the stage, crisscrossed the country by air, rail, highway and thumb, mourned at Wounded Knee, gazed into the eyes of the crow at Grand Canyon, and paid tribute at the grave of Geronimo. He has labored in the fields of plenty, toiled on the assembly line, pursued higher education, and attempted to enlighten children in the public schools. He has been a pilgrim and a seeker of truth. He is married to the love of his life. All the while he has chronicled his thoughts and revelations in words: plays, poetry, novels, stories and essays.

He is the author of *Wasichu: The Killing Spirit* (Crow Dog Press), *Ghost Dance Insurrection* (Dry Bones Press) and the *Jazzman Chronicles* (Crow Dog Press).